CAUTIVOS

CAUTIVOS

Ariel Dorfman

OR Books
New York · London

All rights information: rights@orbooks.com
Visit our website at www.orbooks.com
First printing 2020

Published by OR Books, New York and London

Library of Congress Cataloging-in-Publication Data: A catalog record for this book is available from the Library of Congress.

Typeset by Lapiz Digital Services.

paperback ISBN 978-1-68219-229-0 • ebook ISBN 978-1-68219-230-6

For Angélica, this captive heart of mine that she has freed.

" . . . What I now want to tell you, you must swear to keep a secret until after I am dead.

" . . . . I swear it, Sancho answered."

—*Don Quixote de la Mancha*

CERVANTES CHRONOLOGY

THE EVENTS NARRATED in *Cautivos* begin on September 19th, 1597 and culminate on January 5th and 6th, 1598, a period during which Miguel de Cervantes was unjustly imprisoned for many months in the Sevilla jail.

A brief chronology may help readers to situate this major transition in his life.

1547 (September 29th). Miguel is born in Alcalá de Henares. His family wanders through many cities in the years to come. Sometime between 1554 and 1564, Cervantes studies at the Jesuit Colegio in Sevilla, where he coincides with Pedro de León, the man who, as a priest, will preside years later over the Sevilla jail during Miguel's months there.

1569. Cervantes wounds a petty nobleman in Madrid and flees to Italy, where he enlists as a soldier.

1571. He fights heroically at Lepanto, the pivotal naval battle where Spain and its allies defeat the Turkish fleet. Despite injuries to his lungs and the loss of the use of his left hand, he will see more combat in the next years.

1575. Returning with his brother Rodrigo to Spain, their ship is boarded by Berber pirates. Five harrowing years of captivity in Algiers will ensue.

1580. Having been ransomed and restored to his homeland, he will soon discover that his compatriots do not appreciate or reward his services.

1581. Cervantes accepts an offer from Felipe II's secret service to return to the Barbary Coast as a spy, in order to bring back information about the next moves by Turkey and its supporters in the region. The mission is brief and he will not be further employed in this capacity.

1584. Miguel has some plays (several of them dealing with his captivity) staged in Madrid, with scant success. As a result of an affair with Ana Franca, he fathers an illegitimate daughter, Isabel, whom he will not recognize until several decades have passed. That same year he marries Catalina de Salazar in Esquivias, a small village in La Mancha. The marriage is not a happy one. Miguel will spend many years away from his wife, seeing her only sporadically.

1585. He publishes *La Galatea*, a pastoral novel, that does not result in the fame and fortune he seeks. A scattering of poems here and there do no better.

1587–1597. Miguel engages in two successive jobs in Andalucía: the first, as a commissioner for the King, appropriating oil and wheat from reluctant merchants and peasants; the second, as a tax collector in the same provinces. During that period, he spends a week in jail in Castro del Río in 1592 on trumped up charges.

1597–98. Imprisoned again, this time in the Sevilla jail, due to yet another corrupt magistrate, who blames Cervantes for a debt for which he was not responsible. *Cautivos* takes place in this setting.

1605. First part of *Don Quixote* is published. The novel's instant popularity does not alleviate the poverty in which Cervantes continues to dwell. In June of that year, Miguel and family are in Valladolid, where they are jailed in connection to a nobleman's murder outside their house. Their only crime was trying to help the victim before he died.

1613. Great success of his *Novelas Ejemplares*. Several stories in the book deal with the picaresque low-life he met in the Sevilla jail and elsewhere.

1615. Second part of *Don Quixote* published to still more acclaim.

1616. Cervantes dies, according to most sources, on April 23rd. His funeral has no public relevance whatsoever. Three hundred ninety-nine years later, forensic experts announce that they have found what they believe to be the author's bones, but of this there is no certainty, just as there is none about how *Don Quixote* originated or was written.

As to my own novel about these events, I can only hope that it lives up to the words of Cervantes himself in his masterpiece, when he writes: "Thou hast seen nothing yet."

ONE

" . . . Begotten in a prison, where every discomfort has its place and every sad sound makes its home."

—*Don Quixote de la Mancha*

I WATCH MIGUEL de Cervantes being led into the Cárcel de Sevilla, half pulled and half pushed by rough, burly hands on either side of his hunched body, I watch the scene because there is nothing else I can do, I am condemned to witness this humiliation today, this 19th of September of 1597, just as I have been forced to witness so many other misfortunes since I quietly surfaced by his side all those years ago.

Despite the travails that have beset us and the terrors that lie ahead, I have not lost hope.

A hope that no longer lodges in his heart. It is a matter of gazing on the somber face of our fifty-year-old author and how his shackled legs falter into the prison that is to be his home for unforeseeable dawns. Cervantes knows as I do that there is no escape from this place, not even for someone like him. Such an expert at breaking out of bonds and foiling captors and finding humor even in the direst circumstances, this time these immense walls—they are painted in black from top to bottom—are not to be thwarted.

As black as the door that is about to close behind him.

And as black as the thoughts that invade him, with nothing to hold onto.

And me? I say to him. Hold on to me, I say. You've survived five years of arduous captivity in Algiers without ever bowing your head, Miguel. And always proclaimed that every door that closes announces another door that opens. This current imprisonment in Sevilla is but one more challenge, indeed may promise renewal.

He does not respond. He never responds when I speak to him, insists on not listening to my counsel, will not recognize that I am keeping him company.

I'll admit that this may be the wrong moment to demand that he acknowledge my voice. Not when he is swamped by the stench reeking from the bowels of the building, a lascivious groundswell that can only feed the venom that, year after year, has already been increasing its grip on his inadvertent heart, not when he fears he will be unable to overcome the bitter and taxing test that lies ahead.

His unreceptive mood is soured further by the infernal noise that greets him here, at the threshold, with the *Calle de las Sierpes* behind, the blue sky of Andalucía above him for the last time for who knows how long, the fresh breeze from the Guadalquivir as it drifts towards the sea and breathes a sweet and insolent goodbye to his neck as the clang of the dark door shutters out the light from Sevilla. The bedlam panting at him from inside the prison conjures up for us both a demented dog, an insane asylum, so much chaos and turmoil slapping his skin that I am confounded, it is not clear which of the two is thinking these thoughts, *they must all be crazy, have been rendered wild by the sound of themselves, senselessly shouting their own obsessions without listening to anybody else,* an uproar that is not likely to subside entirely in the months yet to be, not at night, not at dawn, not during prayers, not when an execution is about to take place and all inmates, we have been told, are supposed to be reverent and contrite, the voices may lower to a whisper, but their indocility will never leave his ears, *this is a place where one is never alone, where you cannot hear yourself thinking, where writing is impossible.*

Where writing is impossible.

He is wrong, I wager my incipient life that he is wrong. Life is but one crossroads after another and at each one we must smile and even laugh, if possible. For, what can be funnier than to reach a fork in the road and be certain that both paths will lead to a beating?

So, let's see what confronts us, Miguel, with our head up high.

What confronts us first, just past the arch, is a notary, who consigns the prisoner's name and his crime, then passes him on to the tender mercies of the graying porter who has not bothered to examine anything about this new arrival save the bag he carries, hitched to his right shoulder like a hump.

"D'you know why they call this *La Puerta de Oro,* the golden door?" The attendant gestures towards the blackened gateway. "Because this is where we find out what each man is worth."

Cervantes straightens to his full height, perhaps secretly invigorated by my exhortations, and answers, jocular: "Then it should be called the door of diamonds in my case—I am full of gems."

The porter avidly grabs the bag, dumps the contents on the table in front of him. "Shit," he says. "This is all shit. Gems? If you hid them—just tell me where and—"

"Here," Miguel answers, pointing to his head. "And here," to his heart.

"Swears he's funny, this one," comments one of the constables clutching him, the corpulent, older one who has not washed his teeth in several decades, Cervantes gags each time the man opens the cesspool of his mouth.

"And innocent," adds the second constable, the younger one who has not cleaned his fingernails since he was born, those fingernails do not relent, as they dig into Miguel's skin.

"Like me, a lamb," the porter responds, sifting through the objects, all that Cervantes possesses in the world, settles on a locket and a derelict comb. "Like you and my wife and Padre Pedro de León, bless his soul, all, all, all of us lambs. Though everybody in the flock pays, everybody pays tribute at la Puerta de Oro." He picks up a purse, jingles it so the coins ring out. "Padre de León said to leave you whatever money you were bringing along, said you'd be wanting it—and who am I to deny a holy man, especially if he went to school with you, who am I to deny his advice? But luck can carry you only so far, you'll just have to scratch yourself with your own *uñas*, you'll be needing those gems and diamonds you say are in your head and your heart, though I'd bet they're probably somewhere up your ass. Be needing everything you can peddle, because Padre de León isn't here all week and without a protector . . ."

The cocky expression that Cervantes managed to dress himself with changes, it's bad news that he won't be greeted or guided by his old friend Pedro from the *Colegio de la Compañía de Jesús*. His disappointment is so manifest and forlorn that the porter takes pity on him. "Hey. Padre de León will be back. From time to time the road calls to him to do some good deeds, vanquish evil, thinks he can change the world. Talking the whores of Córdoba into repenting, making sure each bed of the brothel is clean of bugs even if the ladies don't listen to him. I've seen him ministering water and communion to the galley slaves at the port here in Sevilla, he even tried to mediate between two bands of *rufianes* and their slingshots at the *Apedreadero*, such a saint he'd rather receive stones from both sides than have those thugs hurt each other. He wasn't gone but five minutes and they were at it again. Illusions! That's what keeps him, keeps us all, going. And going is what you should be doing. Off, off with you. Be careful, here come the *avispas*. Once they sting a client, they won't let go."

Sure enough, as soon as Cervantes and his two keepers enter the prison itself, he is beset by a *caterva* of *procuradores* offering their services from this flank and that, scurrying up in front of him as he mounts the dank stairs, calling out from each step, like wasps sucking and withering the grapes until the *racimos* are dry. I can barely make out who is who in the cacophony of solicitations: "I'm a friend of the judge and the *escribano*, sir, I'll have you out of here before you can blink an eye." And: "Don't listen to that Judas, what matters here is who knows the warden, the warden's the cousin of my brother-in-law, you'll see how we take care of you." And: "You can start laughing at the world, señor, because the secretary of the court knows me since childhood in Granada." And: "The judge does what I tell him, I know things about him and his three mistresses, oh you just wait and see how we get him to dance to our tune, just trust me, I can represent you for less than this *zángano*, he'd cheat his own grandmother out of her last *maravedí*, that's if he knew who she is, the bastard."

A dust storm of proposals and counterproposals that Cervantes does his best to ignore. Until the horde of barristers, sniffing that this recalcitrant *preso nuevo* is scorning their advances—oh, my Miguel has met so many similar schemers, his life is littered with preening liars and cheats—suddenly spins away from him, they notice a new arrival whose feathers are being plucked at the Golden Door and sprint, almost tumble, almost frolic, down the stairs towards their new quarry. Cervantes allows himself a smile at their folly, at how easy it would have been to fall for their false promises, he smiles at how much better he is than these swindlers at making people believe he is telling the truth when he is hiding so much, things only I am privy to.

That smile fades, along with a smidgen of self-satisfaction as he approaches the second door.

The porter there introduces himself as Urbaldo Rojas, "and this is the *Puerta del Cobre.*" He does not explain what is obvious, that there is less to filch from the prisoner here, that only copper pennies are left, or, in this case, a threadbare shirt which he promptly pockets, along with a cracked mirror. The mirror belonged to Miguel's mother, Leonor de Cortinas, the only thing she bequeathed to him when she died five years ago. He tries not to feel any pain at its loss, concentrating on getting the man to repeat the Cervantes surname right—is the fellow deaf?

Not at all. Urbaldo's a joker, or thinks he is.

"Ciervantes, eh, looks as if someone at home will be growing you some horns while you're away?"

If I had my way, I'd take out my sword and cut the squalid, felonious villain to bits—his mis-pronouncement of the Cervantes patronymic needs to be punished. The butt of these slurs, however, does not take the bait. Unlike me, he has got used to people making fun of his name, seeing as how Cervantes is so close to *ciervo*—and deer, of course, have horns on their head. He has also learned, as I have not, as perhaps I never will, to control himself: in his hothead youth, Miguel got into trouble assailing anyone who dared to make this sort of allusion. So maybe it's fortunate that he doesn't even have a scabbard by his side and only one good hand to turn into a fist. But if I had anything to brandish other than these words, well . . .

That's how it is, nevertheless, no matter how much I hate to admit that I cannot defend him. Only follow his steps as he shuffles along a narrow gallery to the third door, where his shackles will be unlocked and his body assigned to the *calabozo* cell called *Pestilencia*, better than *Miseria* despite its horrid name, according to the ancient gatekeeper, mumbling the explanation as he extricates from Miguel's bag a battered book. It's a copy of *La Galatea,* the pastoral novel Cervantes published more than fifteen years ago, I remember how we celebrated that occasion as if he would reap immortality from its existence.

The old man grunts with delight, purloins the book along with its respective slipcase.

"I am unlettered," he says, "but I love the feel of books. Is this one any good?"

"The best," Cervantes answers, unwilling to reveal that he is its author and that nobody cares, or remembers, or reads it anymore, that this is his last copy and that it does not matter if it is lost, what good will it do him in this penitentiary?

"You assert it with such certainty, sir, that I look forward to having someone read it to me. Maybe you might do me and some other avid listeners the favor some night?"

"If you are interested in goatherds who fall in love with shepherdesses sworn to eternal chastity, if you are not irked by a hermit who goes mad because the focus of his desire disdains his advances, if you like stories of lovers separated by storms and pirates, and verses lamenting the contempt of nymphs and the ups and downs of fortune, then, yes, why not?"

"In truth, sir, begging your pardon, but we prefer books of chivalry," the gatekeeper says, and I can't deny that I vigorously agree with him. "Shepherds are less exciting than a knight battling giants and wizards," he contends, wistfully returning *La Galatea* to Cervantes, but not the slipcase. "We haven't had anyone read to us since Mateo Alemán left a while ago, so if you're willing, the infirmary is where we like to meet every night. We were hoping to read Don Belianís, the second part, as we can't wait to find out how the princesses will be rescued. Ah . . . Now, what's this?"

At the bottom of the increasingly empty bag, he has discovered a bundle of letters tied together with a frayed red string, scraps of paper so moldered by neglect that they hold no apparent value, except perhaps to light a winter fire. "For how long, sir, do you carry these riches with you?"

The man is genuinely curious, the first mild question put to this particular prisoner in many hours, perhaps in days, and Cervantes is softened enough by the sociability of this grizzled, quirky gatekeeper to respond in a voice that I know he reserves for instances when he is telling the truth: "I composed them long ago for friends in Algiers who, like you, sir, did not know how to read or write but wanted to send news home to their families. I promised that I would deliver these messages when I was safe in Spain. Alas, I have not had occasion yet to keep that promise."

"And may God and His Holy Mother keep you alive, sir, till the day that you're able to do so," the man says as he fingers his rosary. "Remember to ask for me, old Ginés, if ever you need something special—like a lass or two when the winter evenings become unbearable. And perhaps you will mount to the infirmary tonight or tomorrow and read a book of chivalry to us? The fee to be negotiated with Papa Pasamonte."

Cervantes knows these books of chivalry all too well and is not, as I am, fond of them, so he avoids committing himself, but makes sure to nod courteously as he turns away from the one man in the last few hours who has blessed him with a sliver of kindness. His feet are now free of chains, but he can't help stumbling, and would fall if not for the two guards who still escort him and urge him forward, one step and then another, into the tumult and gloom and stink of the inner reaches of Hell.

His disarray returns, accompanied this time by the treacherous notion that maybe he should have stayed in Algiers, that he was better off among the Muslim pirates: at least they never punished him for things he had not done. As they were enemies and not fellow countrymen, he always knew where he stood with them, never doubted in captivity how he should comport himself, proud that he never succumbed to despair.

Never lost his dignity.

And what mattered most: full of inspiration and creativity back then, on the Barbary Coast, back then in Northern Africa, on the shores of the Mediterranean.

There were flowers under those ramparts, fragrance in the gardens, a promising future.

He tries not to remember at this rancid moment what he left behind in Algiers, who he left behind there in Algiers, the words he voiced to that perfumed woman as he attempted to convince her to return with him to the homeland where he would be hailed triumphantly, a bright literary star rising. All that was needed was to get back to Spain and its fertile language, the Spain that has now jailed his body yet again, the language which has failed thus far to protect him, one insult and injury after another, culminating in this . . .

Not now, not now. Not a tear, not a suspicion of a tear must be allowed to well up. Of all the malevolent tricks our spirit plays upon us, self-pity is the one most to be lamented.

Ánimo, Miguel. Buckle up, each time you fall off a horse, get back on it, rise up and ride forth, never be disheartened.

He suppresses a sigh with difficulty, and takes the scene in.

A drunken swarm of humanity, a beehive poked by a maniac, an anthill run amok accost his eyes, I see what he sees: everywhere ruffians and beggars, cripples and whores, counterfeiters and *salteadores de caminos*, moving this way and that, skirmishing and disputing, scuffling and brawling, clashing and wrangling, eating and spitting, dancing and drooling, everywhere moans and screams, prayers and curses. Curses, above all, most of them from a crowd that comments as five jailers try to extract a prisoner from a fount of filthy water from where he throws excrement and profanities in equal measure at his pursuers, pressed on by the chorus of *maleantes*. A smaller group surrounds two brutes circling each other with knives, bets come and go as to who will administer the first stab, if the wound will be mortal or superficial, their blades so close to Cervantes that they almost slice him as they parry and thrust. And who is that old fellow calling out from a stall that fresh vegetables and fruit have come in, braised cod can be had at yesterday's price? And can it be, to one side, half in the shadows, a gigantic bearded *valentón* with a shining bald pate fondles the breasts of two women, who calmly coo a song of love, while a young lad decants wine into his mouth, can it be that Miguel de Cervantes has been condemned, through no fault of his own, no fault save his honesty and habitual bad luck, to this pandemonium?

He had been told by friends, he had been warned by his boyhood friend Padre de León, how bad things were, but those cautions had hardly registered, he never thought he would have to cross that black door of the Sevilla jail. Even after the *corchetes* had burst into his room in Tomás Gutierrez's inn and read the order from that idiotic judge Gaspar de Vallejo, even once his feet had been bound in chains and he had to endure the shame of staggering through those streets he loved so well amid the jeers of strangers, even during that endless, humiliating march he had fooled himself into imagining that somehow the experience ahead of him would be like Castro del Río exactly five years ago, that September 19, 1592.

That previous incarceration in Castro del Río had spoiled him.

The townspeople had given him a hero's welcome. They knew Cervantes well, from previous visits as the King's commissioner when, instead of squeezing from them every last morsel that they owned, he had negotiated a deal that had staved off imminent hunger and hardship. They especially remembered how, on one of those occasions, he had confronted Jaime Moreno, a *sacristán* who was hoarding tons of food in his granary. Rather than agreeing to the cleric's demand that the King's commissioner confiscate the last shafts of wheat and drops of oil from the famine-struck peasants and merchants, Cervantes had proceeded, with my inaudible *beneplácito*, to jail the covetous Moreno. So, when the Archbishop of Córdoba reacted by excommunicating the said apostate Miguel de Cervantes, the residents of Castro del Río ignored the postings on the walls of the Iglesia de la Asunción commanding that nobody was to have dealings with this devil who had dared to sequester ecclesiastical property. He was the town favorite, their savior—and was greeted as such when Francisco de Moscoso's warrant for his detention happened to catch up with Cervantes precisely at Castro del Río, the best of places to be arrested.

Arrested, in a manner of speaking.

Antonio Hoyas, the warden in charge of his imprisonment, gave an especially warm welcome to the man who, some years before, had saved that warden's simple, hardworking brother from ruin. If it was inevitable that Cervantes spend the night in the enormous basement of the Ayuntamiento that officiated as the town jail, nothing prevented Hoyas from giving the accused permission, as soon as dawn peeped over the hills surrounding Castro del Río, to amble up and down the streets to his heart's content. So long, Hoyas cautioned, that you don't step outside our fortress-like walls.

I loved watching Miguel climb to the very top of the town, walking the ramparts of the old castle—and there, below him, below us, field upon field, row upon row, of olive trees snaking along knolls and hummocks like gnarled warriors. And all those other trees: *tasajo, olmo, álamo, chopo, fresno, encina* and the pungent medicinal smell of eucalyptus, and the sight of *tórtolas* migrating and partridges and *alcaravanes* feeding on the river banks, and one solitary owl that he prayed would visit him and hoot next to his cell one of these solitary nights, lamenting the lost mate that would never return. And the muddy Guadajoz flowing towards the glorious waters of the Guadalquivir amid the remains of Roman aqueducts and *túmulos.* Then down the alleys, all those white houses and people he couldn't remember having met inviting him into their homes and gardens, one afternoon he helped an old woman—oh yes, my gallant Miguel—transplant a *zarzamora,* begging her pardon for being so clumsy, mentioning that he had lost the use of the other hand at Lepanto. It turned out she had lost two sons in that battle that had converted the Mediterranean into a Spanish sea, and they had cried together, and then smiled later, when they discovered Egyptian coins from who knew what bygone era under the bush he had uprooted.

Oh, how he had enjoyed those days of leisure, oh how happy I was for him. And for me. I had been keeping a wary eye on him. As he dabbled in ventures that led nowhere year after year, I trained myself not to be irked by how long my gestation was taking, and therefore reasonably nursed a twinge of hope that now that he was finally forced to stop wandering, this confinement in Castro del Río would be the interlude he needed to cool his heels and sharpen and inflame his inspiration.

Why should I not yearn for such a reprieve, hope that a bout of forced repose might move him to start writing again?

Perhaps that very night?

But then, as the sun set, back to the Ayuntamiento and his cellar, where a hot meal awaited the honored guest—*albóndigas* and *bizcochos*, *choricillos* and *morcillas*, *flamenquines* and rabbit stew. And wine, of course, never lacking, as after the meal, the town worthies would drop by—even a priest or two came along, they had also hated that *sacristán* Moreno who gave them all a bad name, and fortunately the son of a bitch was long gone, reassigned to who knows what unfortunate diocese, and all these visitors would ridicule the inept magistrate Moscoso who was illegally demanding restitution—from the King's commissary, no less—of three hundred *fanegas* of wheat, plus 175 *reales* for court costs. This Moscoso was a fool and on the take and so blind—here the laughter noticeably notched up—that he didn't realize his young, supple wife, kept under lock and key in Écijas, was turning him into a *cornudo* every chance she got with the *mulatillo* who was supposed to guard her. Served him right: he had only been able to marry the unwilling girl, because he had showered her avaricious parents with the corrupt money he received from exercising . . . . What? And here the neighbors would all shout "*justicia*" as if it were an insult rather than something to be devotedly desired. And once they had mocked Moscoso and played some cards and danced some local *jarchas*, the stalwarts who were too drunk to straggle home would ask Miguel about his years as a captive in Algiers and the strange customs of the Moors and was it true that their veiled women loved to do you know what and where and how with Christian slaves? And the night would end with the prisoner regaling his *comensales* with comical tales of his many years on the run-down roads of Andalucía collecting wheat and oil for the King's Invincible Armada and then tax arrears and how he had always favored the poor and tried to be a scourge of the rich, and, he said, "such attempts at redress are what have brought me to be your reluctant lodger in this sweet jail of Castro del Río." And I listened attentively to all those stories from my shadows, eager for the day when they would find an audience that far surpassed this trifling crowd in one tiny town.

Those days, six, maybe they had been seven, felt more like a vacation than a penance, so that he had almost regretted it, as I certainly had, my designs for the renaissance of his artistic ambitions again postponed, when his boss Isunza intervened from the remoteness of Madrid to get the unfair arrest warrant lifted and that bumbler Moscoso reprimanded. Yes, I admit to regretting the hour when Cervantes was released. Would that he had stayed among those hearty souls forever. An experience of peace and quiet that he has never forgotten, that he still pines for.

No wonder then that he had wanted to persuade himself that the Sevilla penitentiary would be a larger and benevolent replica of Castro del Río, no wonder that now, five years later, on this September day of 1597, he is bemused by the patio bedlam in front of his eyes and disappointed by his own penchant for delusions, why did he keep substituting his desires for reality, till when would he continue to set himself up for regrets and bruisings and betrayals, leading, finally, to this demonic place from which there is no escape.

"Here you are," says the younger *corchete*. "Home at last."

The two policemen let him go, take a step back, do not ditch their charge yet. They must be curious to see how this one will fare as soon as he is not under their protection, they look forward to watching what—and who, and who—is about to descend upon this Miguel de Cervantes in this patio, even before he is dragged to the cell he will share from now on with thirty other convicts.

A surprise is in store for these two onlookers. And for me.

"Newcomer," someone heaves out and the word is fervently repeated by all the detainees, hurtling out of the dusk of the central patio, *newcomer, newcomer, newcomer,* until suddenly all is stillness, even the ruffian waist-deep in the fountain stops cursing and sweeping filth at his jailers, even the two who are dueling with knives delay their quarrel, the scroungers and prostitutes and pickpockets make way for the gigantic hulk of the bald and bearded *valentón,* who has risen from the enjoyment of the breasts of his two damsels, he stands up and the reeking waves of inmates promptly part for him, as if he were Moses.

He stands in front of Miguel de Cervantes, does not ask his name, cares not a whit what sins the new prisoner is purging in this place of penance, sizes him up at a glance, seems to know more about what this prisoner may be worth than the prisoner himself, the ogre is only interested in one thing.

"Good for what?" he asks. "Tell Papa Pasamonte the truth."

Cervantes hesitates. Has he forgotten his vocation, the words that he consoled himself with in Algiers when death appeared to be imminent, that a remote woman once breathed as a goodbye? Having kept faith since then, despite each wrong turn in the road, despite each abhorrently miserable misfortune, is this the moment to doubt who he is, the person he hopes to someday become? I sigh and mutter to him, mouth the answer before he speaks, give him courage, tell him that I am proud of him, I am glad to be part of his tomorrows, his infinite and many tomorrows, if only, if only he can respond, if only . . .

"I'm a writer," he says. "I write, that's what I do."

"And what do you write about?"

Now Cervantes does not hesitate. "Love and death," he says. "What else is there to write about?"

It is the perfect response—though I would have added justice, I would have liked him to add the adventure of justice—and now he does, "And the adventure of justice," he says, maybe thinking of the company he now inadvertently keeps, and I feel satisfied and hopeful, and what comes next elates me even more.

Because the monster smiles. And then embraces him, takes Cervantes into both his arms, wraps those colossal coils around the man who will someday be known, if I have anything to do with it, as the author of the greatest novel in the history of the world.

"Just the man we need," he murmurs into Cervantes's ear, and the gentleness of those words wipe out—though never completely—the mayhem engulfing and soiling the air of the Cárcel de Sevilla. And then repeats the words out loud for all to hear: "Just the man we need, you fuckers, just the man we need." He turns and gestures towards a slight bedraggled sorrowful man in a corner of the courtyard. "Alonzo Ballesteros! Alonzo, you lucky son of a bitch, you can fuck my mother if I'm wrong. These bastards won't hang you three days from now without words to help you on your way. And this fellow might even get you off scot-free if he's as good as he thinks he is, as able as Papa Pasamonte believes he is, more than the Credo. Isn't that so, writer?"

And Miguel de Cervantes realizes with relief that once again he will find a way to survive.

As for me, I will wait—who knows until when, the thought strikes me that my patience might run out, my destiny dry up, that one day I may simply disappear and fade into nothingness forever—as for me, like so many unknown and unfinished creatures of my sort, I will keep waiting for as long as I can for the moment of my birth to find its way into the light.

TWO

"Freedom, Sancho, is one of the most precious gifts that the heavens bestowed on men; no treasures buried in the earth or the sea can equal it; for freedom, as for honor, one can and must risk life and, in contrast, captivity is the worst evil that can befall men."

—*Don Quixote de la Mancha*

FOR SOMEONE LIKE me, months pass quickly, I am still here at the start of 1598, still keeping our Miguel company in the freezing winter of the Sevilla jail, even if he has only the mildest intimations of my existence.

I watch him awaken this morning of January 5th like every morning, hoping, as I always do, that we will soon have a radiant meeting of minds. A confidence that, admittedly, I try to bolster each dawn, but today could be the day, today I am more intrepid than usual, forcefully predicting, despite the cold that is chilling my author's bones, that something decisive will occur.

Maybe my hope is shored up by the conviction that here in jail things have been coming along smoothly, my plans and his plans inching towards each other, helping me to grope towards the meaning of who I am, what lot awaits me. My full emergence has been exasperatingly slow, because it depends on my Miguel resolving a battle between sadness and joy that has raged within him since childhood, a conflict that, in this unlikeliest of places, seems to be finding some sort of outcome, his spirit bending evermore towards the light, a process that has advanced night after night and day after day without major setbacks.

Until now, until right now, right this minute, when, like the bubonic plague, those three men erupt into the Cárcel de Sevilla threatening to twist his dreams and make them into nightmares, stop us in our tracks. He notices the trio blustering their way into the central visitors' hall of this enormous prison, he shudders as, from the corner of his unmoored spectacles and weak eyes, he confirms that they are abruptly, irrevocably, resentfully slithering towards him, Marín and Garrido and Carrasco, bursting forth yet again into his life.

And into mine, into mine.

For nigh eighteen years, their memory has haunted me. I cannot forget them or their words, the first harsh words I ever heard in my existence.

October 31st of the year of our Lord 1580.

How could I forget the day they appeared and blackened our lives, the day that Miguel de Cervantes touched the soil of Spain after his long Algerian captivity, that was it, that was when, as soon as he sank to his knees on the beach in Valencia and kissed the ground, that was it, that was the moment chosen for me to emerge from oblivion.

I did not know why I was suddenly there nor who I was, but it was immediately clear, as the waves of the Mediterranean sounded behind us, that my fate was linked forever to the fate of the man quietly thanking God for his liberation.

There I was, barely fluttering into consciousness, nameless and without a body to call my own, induced to faintly surface by that initial breath of his motherland, there I was, the instant that he filled his lungs with his country's pungent, matchless air, the unmistakable smell of hash and lentils that some woman was cooking nearby on the beach and that he recognized instantly in spite of those endless days and nights of absence, that air and that smell must have been what stimulated my spectral appearance, lured me into his world, gave me permission to settle close by him, start to reside inside the home of his heart.

And as soon as my mind came up with that word, the word home, I understood that was it, the reason, it was his homecoming that had called me forth from whatever nightfall I had inhabited till then.

And thus it was that, having taken up lodgings in the life of Miguel de Cervantes, I awaited the next moment, when he would cease to pray, when he would stand up and reveal to me what my quest was to be, when I would be able to reveal myself to him, both of us seeking a new hearth of words together, together and in each other.

Nothing occurred. Or rather, *they* occurred, three long shadows grew on the sand and shore of Valencia, three long shadows blotted out the evening sun.

Cervantes lifted his eyes and I saw what he saw, that unholy trinity looming above him—and I heard what he heard, their summons to come with them.

"We have some questions to ask you, Miguel de Cervantes."

He did not have time for me, he did not have peace for me, for me or anything else. His concentration was focused elsewhere: why this unwelcome, why were they taking him into a dark room, what would they do to him if his answers were not suitable, why him, why him?

I did have time for him though, all the time and peace in the world. I trailed my newfound friend like a devoted dog, kept hovering bird-like by his side, determined that my attentiveness—unacknowledged though it might be—might offer some hushed comfort during the interrogation he was about to endure.

"Name?"

As soon as they pushed Cervantes down on a rickety chair, Marín spat out that first question.

Name? They wanted to know his name? Was this a tactic? Perhaps an attempt to intimidate their victim, gauge if he was willing to humiliate himself by accepting their right to ask him something they obviously already knew, as they had come to snare him on the beach because he was none other than the selfsame Miguel de Cervantes.

"Name?" The repetition, salivated with more urgency, friction, danger.

How would Cervantes react? No matter how much in the dark I was regarding his identity at that early point in our association, this much was certain: I would not have been assigned to anyone who gave in easily to tactics of terror, not me, not for me to be partnered for life with someone easily harassed. So I was therefore delighted when the man who held my destiny in his hands answered, sarcastically, defiantly: "Who do you think I am?"

"The respondent refuses to give his name." Marín turned to Carrasco, who squatted on a stool next to the table, quill at the ready: "Write that down, notary. Write down that he is obdurate and inflexible and recalcitrant, and that he must, therefore, be hiding something."

"Hiding something for sure," Garrido, standing directly behind Cervantes, hissed the next words into his ear. "More than something."

"I told you it was going to be a long night," said Marín. "Didn't I tell you this one would be a tough nut to crack?"

"Oh, he'll crack, they all crack."

Marín grabbed one of Miguel's shoulders, Garrido dug into the other one, and who knows what would have followed if Carrasco had not piped up. "All we're asking, sir, is that you confirm your name for the record. It's standard procedure. Please, gentlemen, give our guest the chance to respond."

For a while, all that the five of us in that room, five if you include me, that is, could hear was the drip drip drip of water, from the wall or maybe a bucket filled to overflow crouched in a corner or—and then Cervantes broke the silence as if he were breaking a bone or a tooth.

"I have nothing to hide," Cervantes said. "My father is the honorable Rodrigo de Cervantes and he and my mother, Leonor, baptized me as Miguel and that is what everybody, just like you, call me."

Had he given them this answer because the notary had expressed the request in a soft, respectful way? Or was it that, after years in foreign dungeons, he simply wanted to get this over with, stop playing hide and seek with these thugs, feel the free air of Valencia freshen his face, go out there and listen to the townspeople speaking Spanish, did he want to seek somebody like me out and start his new life?

Whatever the reason, a mistake. A mistake, I thought, to give men like these even the slightest satisfaction, they'll only take that as a sign of weakness.

That my fears were swiftly borne out gave me no satisfaction. I had to witness how that innocent response was greeted with hilarity by Garrido, while Marín started sniffing his prey like a dog, up and around and down to the crotch. But amazingly, instead of crushing the nose his tormentor was wrinkling with distaste, Cervantes added—another mistake, to defend oneself like that, justify what needs no justification—that he was a *cristiano viejo*, a Christian of pure, old, proven blood, certified through all four grandparents.

A mistake, a mistake, a mistake, how can you not realize that—?

And then I stopped. What was my incessant disparagement accomplishing? This was not only a test for him. It was a test for me. Did I trust Miguel de Cervantes? Did I trust that he knew what he was doing, that he had a plan? Had he not survived up till now without my assistance? Was I to be one of those who fled when the going got rough, turned his back on a friend and betrayed him? Or would I stick it out through thick and through thin, would I be his steadfast sidekick?

If Cervantes needed to publicly defend his lineage, I had to respect that.

Marín, of course, was not bound by any such constraints or courtesies. He withdrew from his sniffing expedition, and let out a loud yawn. "Yeah, yeah, yeah. Everybody's got certificates, affidavits, letters galore. Who cares if your father goes by the name of Cervantes. Who knows if he's even your father. What matters here, what always matters, is the mother. Leonor? Ah, but her surname? Cortinas. Seems like a Jewish name, Cortinas, don't you think? Jews worship curtains, so they can draw them shut and perform their blood rites far from inquisitive eyes, a proven fact. When I was a kid, I hid behind one, a curtain, plush and heavy, made believe I was a Jew, saw what adults didn't want me to know, that's what started me on the path to rooms like this one. Where I can poke behind the curtains of each man's soul."

"Hey," Garrido said, blowing his nose and cleaning his fingers on Marín's shirt, "we haven't got time for your childhood memories. We're interested in his memories, whatever the Hell his name is."

"If he has memories, that is. Of his own childhood, I mean. I mean, where were you born, and when?"

Finally, a question that interested me! They were making believe they knew nothing about him when, in fact, they must have had ample and meticulous intelligence. This was one more job for them, all in a night's work, as far as I could tell, part of their routine duties, to protect the fatherland by weeding out from the thousands of returning captives any renegade who had relinquished Christ for the idolatry of Islam and might be bent on sowing terror. And this Cervantes, just another fellow to be grilled. And then off to supper or a wife or a lover or some ale in the local tavern till it was somebody else's turn tomorrow.

Whereas I, whereas I . . . I had no wife to go home to, no tavern to drink myself senseless, no-one else's tomorrow to look forward to.

Without Miguel de Cervantes, I was nothing.

Without Miguel de Cervantes, I did not have a chance at existence, not a stab at existence, not a flicker of a possibility of existing.

And yet, at that early stage, there in Valencia eighteen years ago, I knew hardly anything about him, my loyalty an act of blind faith, save that this man was the master of my future. What made it so difficult to judge him was that I could only hazard guesses about the years that Miguel de Cervantes had lived without me. Like anyone who meets a new acquaintance, I would be obliged to piece together this stranger's past and his personality from scraps of conversation, the figs and figments that he enacted for others, wade through the contradictory versions he presented of himself, tiny moments when he disclosed some buried truth. As if I were reading about a character in a novel or watching him act on a platform.

From a discrete and loving distance.

Because whatever gods had enticed me from oblivion had astutely imposed strict limits on our relationship. Conditions that forced me to linger by him deferentially, hang on his every word, the iron rules that governed my existence mandating that only when I had watched him as he ate and defecated, slept and made love, it was only then, once closeness had been earned by keen and incessant surveillance, that I would be allowed to cautiously enter the premises of his body. Slowly, slowly, so he will not panic, will not apprehend that he has been invaded, let him evolve naturally towards the moment when he would fully meet me. Differentiating me from the start from those three horrible intruders bent on violating his privacy.

Even so, I was grudgingly beholden to those insolent men for giving me the opportunity to eavesdrop and discover as much as I could about my author's biography. It was news to me, in fact, when and where he had been born and thus his weary answer, "Alcalá de Henares, September 29th, 1547," was music to my ears.

Not that I was given much chance to enjoy that music, mull over this new madrigal of evidence. Garrido made sure about that, asking something far more fundamental. "So tell me. When you were born, did you know that you were going to be a writer? That's what rumor has it, that's what people say you always wanted to be, is that true?"

"Is poetry a crime now?" Cervantes asked.

"Well, here's some advice, whether your dear mother's name is Cortinas, or was Cortinas, or will be Cortinas, or who knows what else, here's some friendly advice. You'd better cultivate patience."

"If I could sell a small quota of the patience I have accumulated," Cervantes said, smiling sadly, "I'd be rich enough to make sure somebody like you did not greet me so cordially on the day I finally gain my freedom. When one has been a slave, he learns that patience is the father of all virtue. *Paciencia y barajar.*"

"Words of wisdom," Garrido said. "Never hurry. Because you'd damn well better learn some forbearance if you want to be an author who isn't governed by what's fashionable. Just look at the trash people are reading! You know what they're reading? Nothing's changed in the years you've been away. Books of chivalry, that's what!"

I was indignant at this attack, expecting my new friend Cervantes to defend those fabulous novels packed with feats and exploits, though only later did I realize that my favorable opinion was not rooted in any real experience, as I had not read even one word of those books. And yet I instinctively felt they were endearingly close to me. It was clear that Cervantes, however, did not share my fondness, as he pointedly did not rebuke Garrido. It was Marín who objected, astonishing me, I never thought I could agree with anything uttered by such a detestable scoundrel: "Hey, I like them. I read *Amadís de Gaula* whenever I get a chance. My wife loves the episode where the hero, rejected unfairly by Oriana, goes mad and exiles himself to la Peña Pobre to do penance."

"That's one of the best episodes, absolutely," the notary Carrasco concurred. "But *Amadís* is not my wife's favorite. She prefers *Don Belianís*. Though she's crazy about all books of chivalry."

"Books of shit, not chivalry," Garrido interjected forcefully, and I felt like giving him a good cuff. "Poisoning the public. So, Señor Cervantes or Ciervantes or whatever your name is, if you wish to leave your mark on literature, first lesson: not to rush, rush, rush. But when you were born . . . ?"

"When I was born?"

"He means," Carrasco explained from the shadows, he seemed to be more well-mannered than his two rude companions, "when you were born, were you in a hurry then?"

"Were you anxious to taste life and fame, make a name for yourself, were you? And when the Hell were you born and when?"

"I already told you."

"So you did. But you don't look as if you're thirty-three years old," Marín observed, and I unwillingly had to acquiesce, he looked rather run down in my opinion, much too thin, "that's why my dear Garrido here repeated the question. Are you sure you haven't forged that date of birth to seem akin to our Lord who gave his life on the cross so we sinners could live eternally? Some of us, that is, those who have kept the faith."

The notary again intervened, again siding with Cervantes: "That's the date we have in our records. The day of San Miguel. Makes sense. He aged, that's all. They age, you know, out there, over there. Five years of cruelty, far from home."

"Was the treatment that cruel?" Who asked that, Marín or Garrido? My head was spinning, I was dizzy from this session, so unexpected, so different from what I had supposed would be my host's first day of liberty in his homeland, our first day to serenely get acquainted.

"That's the real question. If you received any favors there, that helped you, so to speak, to survive."

"I tried to escape four times."

Carrasco dutifully wrote the number down. "You said four, right? Yes, that's what our informants report. He's telling the truth about that, at least. His fellow captives—well, most of them—mention his Christian virtue and chastity, no ugly habits or bad associations. Spotless."

"As I can attest through witnesses who swore in Algiers before I left—twenty-five of them in a report that was certified by a notary like you who—"

"Twenty-four," Carrasco corrected him.

"Who cares if they were twenty-four," Garrido said, "or twenty-four hundred and three. What matters is that not one of those witnesses is here in Spain, right, so we can verify that they're telling the truth? Right?"

"They're still captive," said Cervantes. "How can they be here?"

"And yet, here you are," Garrido insisted, "free. And nothing wrong with you. Not maimed, not buried in the desert outside Algiers, not impaled on a stake, not hung from a scaffold, not burnt alive, no sign of two thousand strokes on your feet as your master threatened, ears and nose intact, here you are, unless you are not Miguel de Cervantes."

"If I'm not, then I'd appreciate it if your worships could find the real one. I'm curious to know what mischief that evil twin of mine has been doing in my name."

"He thinks he's a wit, this Miguel de Cervantes."

"And Cortinas. Don't forget the Cortinas."

"Miguel de Cervantes Cortinas. Unscratched. Unscathed."

Carrasco protested: "His hand . . ."

Garrido gave a sympathetic nod. "Lost at Lepanto, serving our good King Felipe and God's Holy Church against the Turk, oh we're not here to deny that epic performance on that great day when the Sultan's fleet was destroyed, cooped the infidel in the Mediterranean. We salute you, we celebrate you, we praise you. Except for one question."

"One little question," said Marín. "How did you manage? In Algiers?"

Manage? Manage what? I asked myself.

"Manage what?" Cervantes asked, as if he were reading my mind.

"Manage five years without having sex. Because you didn't have sex, did you, during these five years? Or did you with . . . who? Moorish sluts? Captured, virtuous Christian damsels? Or with the men who owned them? With their tender, bearded women? Young sodomite boys, all garmented with rich clothes and painted lips?"

I admit to blushing at this, I really did not know how to react. Fortunately, Cervantes did.

"You forgot how I dressed like a woman and hid in a harem. You forgot Hassan Pasha, the King of Algiers, got me pregnant and I gave birth to the Emperor of Trapisonda. Oh. And you forgot donkeys and camels and cats."

"Didn't I tell you he's a wit? Hey, you like to joke, we like to joke. It was just a joke, Miguel de Cervantes, just a joke to see how you responded."

"But we would still like to know how you managed, a strapping young stud like you. In case anyone finds himself in that situation, you know, five years away from home and full of natural appetites, how to manage. And all around you . . ."

"Because Muslims don't think fornication is a sin. Even their mullahs fuck with everything in and out of sight. But this isn't our last meeting, friend, oh no. So, there'll be plenty of time for you to illuminate us on this and so much more. For now, we'll call it quits, eh, Marín?"

"Yes, I'm tired," Marín agreed. "And Carrasco here, his hand must be more cramped than if he'd been doing you know what with it. So, you can go, Miguelito. You must have somebody who kicked the bucket while you were away—and look, it's already the Day of the Dead. And we have our own cemeteries to visit, wives and children to spend time with. So, off with you."

And that was when I realized, as the dawn crept uncertainly through the solitary befouled window of that hovel on that first of November of 1580, that I had chosen my host well, or he had chosen me, I realized that it would be a privilege to wait as long as it took, a privilege to be his companion, however undetectable I might be for now, that's when he stood up and put his one good hand on his one good sword and looked all three of them up and down, up and down, back and forth, until you could have sliced the silence.

"Not yet," Miguel de Cervantes said, very low his voice, all the more alarming because it was not raised in anger. "You want to know what happened? You want to poke around in my soul? You want to open the curtains of my captivity?"

And then he spoke up, finally showing those men who he was, then he spoke words, that night in Valencia eighteen years ago, he spoke words that must still resound today in their memory as they do in mine.

You want the truth, you're salivating for it? Then—no interruptions. Not a whisper. Not one whisper until I'm done. Just one syllable from you or you and especially from you and—my left hand may be crippled from the battle wounds of Lepanto but the right hand is still able to wield a sword as I did in the high seas, under the command of Don Juan de Austria. You may have heard of the scar I inflicted when I was so much younger on that scoundrel Sigura who dared to insult the honor of a lady in my presence, even if it meant banishment to Italy, what I did to him and later to so many others on the battlefield, that will I do to your faces and much more, damn the consequences, and you will be the ones visited by widows and orphans in the cemetery on this Day of the Dead.

Be glad I have indeed nurtured patience.

Given that you seem to know so much about me, you must also know that I have heard questions like yours, slurs worse than yours, back there in Algiers, questions about who I was and what I was worth and who had helped me in my plans to escape and what I was really plotting. Though they pressed me hard, I never revealed what truly mattered, the plots I was indeed hiding, what I would have gladly transmitted to you gentlemen if you had shown the slightest interest. But you did not ask me about the fortifications in Algiers that I know so well, each rampart I have measured, each blockhouse and tower, inch by inch, brick by brick, and how there is a blind spot in the southern castle wall that can be easily breached, you did not ask how many of the 25,000 captives are ready to revolt if Spain were but to send a signal. Nor are you concerned that I never ceased dreaming of this Spain minute by minute in the dankest cellars and the pestilent streets of Algiers.

Five years of chains, five years of dreams, and I come home to this? To you? To men like you who have not seen combat and who have not been captured by pirates nor despaired of ever hugging their family again, men like you asking someone like me if I really was Miguel de Cervantes Cortinas, if my mother's surname did not evoke Jewish heritage and thus impure blood, demanding, of me, of me, that I prove I had not converted to Islam, that I explain how I had survived as a slave in North Africa for so long without betraying my faith, five years without sex, how did I manage, how did I manage?

I arrived in Algiers and it was as if I had entered the mouth of Hell—dark, dark, worse because the sun was beating down on us, the sky was clear and blue, the city sparkled like a jewel. Dark, those dark-skinned urchins shouting against Don Juan of Austria, shouting to us Don Juan, Don Juan, not come here, not come here to rescue you. Die here, Christian dog, die here. A song for my birthday. It was September 29, 1575, and I was 28 years old. And trying not to curse my birth. Murmuring to someone or something still alive inside me, This captivity has been sent as a test, a way of forcing me to give birth to myself as if I were my mother on her bed of suffering, my mother who was soon to learn that her two

sons, Miguel and Rodrigo, had been taken prisoner by the Berbers
and would spend the rest of their lives as slaves unless they were
ransomed, my mother who would spend the eternal nights ahead
imagining the foulest horrors descending on her boys, spend the
days scrounging for every last penny for our ransom.

Though she knew me well enough, must have guessed I was
already searching for a way out. A way out? The endless waters
behind us, the infinite wastelands of sand on three sides, the ramparts blotting the horizon, what horizon? And I carried on my
person two letters vouching for me to Felipe II. One from his half-
brother, that very same Don Juan, and the other from the Duke of
Sessa. More fool I. Trying to get those grandees for whom I was no
more than a blur to recommend me to His Majesty for some succulent post, making believe that they meant something, those letters
that some idiot secretary had written at my behest and signed by
those potentates without a second thought, and here I was, where
my boundless ambition and desire for advancement had landed
me, flaunting my wartime deeds and mutilated left hand, here I
was. Those exaggerated letters, instead of obtaining favors from
our sainted Monarch, caused the infidels who worship Muham-
mad to consider me a man of singular importance. To be redeemed
like a prince. While my family went penniless, forced to sell off the
dowry of my sisters and the bed of my grandparents, and eat stale
bread and take out loan after loan, trying to accumulate funds
that were always vastly insufficient.

So, what was I to do? Plan my escape. Once my master let me
roam the restricted streets within the restricted walls to beg for
food—I'm not going to feed you, Christian dog, forage for yourself, seek alms if your family is too avaricious to rescue you—I used
the skills and wits God gave me to find contacts, fellow hostages,

anyone who could offer assistance. Not easy to tell friend from foe in a city teeming with vendors selling stolen goods, foreign merchants out to make a fortune, corsairs, renegades, veiled women and maimed men.

First try. 1576. Men and women alike would wander in and out of my master's courtyard—where I would stage playlets for the prisoners' amusement, a safe way of having a laugh at our captors. One day I noticed a tall Moor of pale and noble countenance who knew enough Spanish from trading with our Christian merchants to be regaled, even if it was at his expense.

I began to cultivate his friendship.

One day: Will you guide me and four other hidalgos to Orán, the Spanish fort in Orán? His response: For money, sir, for money, and because your brilliance should make the world smile beyond these walls. And the Koran, sir, it says that we should compete with one another in doing good. Wise words, cheap words from someone of faint heart. Two days into the wilderness, surrounded by jackals and buzzards and nomads with eyes like scalpels hunting for escapees, that Moor forsook us. And we had to retreat, myself and my companions. Back in Algiers, the renegade Greek who owned my body but not my soul chained me to the floor of his cellar for many months. An outcome preferable to death, for which there is no remedy, but I was not out of danger, far from it.

The dank, reeking conditions of that dungeon infected my lungs—already sapped by the chest wounds suffered at Lepanto— and they had to carry me to a Moorish hospital, where we were packed three to a bed, if that broken cot could be called with such an august name. On either side of me, two former soldiers were dying of dysentery. Their groans and diarrhea only ceased when dawn and extinction arrived, along with the guards whose task every morning was to drag the corpses to the cemetery. I had just enough strength in one leg to lift it slightly, so the chains clinked. I was alive, that sound said, I'm alive, that is all that separated me from being buried, from suffocating in a common grave. And that is all, gentlemen, that in effect separates us from death: that clink clink our chains make, the bell of our soul announcing our time has not come, and back there in Algiers reminding me that as long as I had a clink clink of strength, as long as I could lift a leg, as long as I can make a bit of noise, there is hope. As soon as I recovered from my illness—thanks be given to angels of mercy—I began planning my next escape.

Here in Sevilla eighteen years later, I can still hear him, still admire his performance as I did on that first dawn together, I was enchanted then, totally absorbed by that flair of his to tell a tale, mesmerized by how he had stayed alive and outwitted his abductors. Not only, for me, a way of learning about the past, but proof of how his silver tongue and sheer creativity and enormous charm had seen him through those dire straits. This bravura enactment that inaugural *amanecer* vindicated my early, blind confidence in him, assured me it was alright for my future to depend on his narrative skills.

As for those three men—wearied by years of listening to an array of drab and dreary and gloomy chronicles of woe told without *gracia*—they must have been pleased, despite his initial aggressiveness, to be thus entertained. They may even have appreciated, felt relief, that an artist, by pulling them into the drastic perspective of *someone who had been there*, could suspend their customary cynical disbelief, perhaps they also remember now, as I do, so many years later in the Sevilla jail, that Cervantes is not among those who give up easily.

I did not give up easily. Second try, 1577: my family sent some money, though not enough to ransom me. I negotiated with the friars to let my brother Rodrigo return to Spain in my place. Before he left I told him what to do: Pay, brother, for a frigate in Valencia that will rescue us, at that beach where we used to walk, there, on the outskirts of Algiers. That was the place I pinpointed for the operation. Near a garden, tended to by Juan, a gardener from Navarra, who befriended me the afternoon I sneaked in to steal some fruit, peaches as sweet as a woman's skin, the women I could only touch in my dreams. Juan was a simple man but wise in his way, spicing up each conversation with a mouthful of proverbs and folk sayings, a stalwart Christian so loyal and naïve and ready to serve that he showed me a cave he had discovered next to the shore. That's where I hid fifteen fellow captives—never did I try to escape alone, always concerned about others, always. I scavenged for food, medicine, clothes, for the seven months they were there, waiting for the boat—only joined them the last few days. Alas, the sailors of that frigate were caught and panicking at this, a renegade of our band who'd sworn he wanted to return to Spain and the true faith of Christ betrayed our cause, and two nights later janissaries on horse and on foot stormed into the cave. I told my friends: I will take the blame, I will tell Hassan Pasha, the king of Algiers, that I am the sole author of this enterprise.

Hassan looked me over with his penetrating, covetous eyes. My naptuk *hung in the balance. My fortune. He was Venetian, I spoke to him in the tongue he had first heard in lullabies: It is my duty, great lord, to escape, and yours, to punish me, but also your privilege to show mercy. A gamble. It worked. I'll have you* beaten to death, two thousand blows on the feet and the belly. He didn't mean it. He had something else in store for me. I was led to the garden by the sea—where a spectacle of terror lay in wait. Juan Navarra, the gardener who had kept us safe, had been strung up with hooks and ropes to a tree while Agi Morato, Juan's owner, watched with cruel eyes and gave orders to mercenaries to continue tormenting my friend. I saw him die slowly, strangled, coughing blood. Would he recant? Would he confess all the details of our plan? For a few seconds his eyes were on my eyes, inside my eyes, calling for me to—what could I do? He gave his soul to heaven and I am alive today to tell his tale, I lived and planned a new escape.

1578. A Moor I trusted and charmed with stories of rewards untold, dukedoms and islands to be his, if he accompanied me on my adventures, this man carried a letter of mine to don Martin de Córdoba, the governor of Orán. Please send a spy who can guide us to freedom. Or officers, I implied, who might lead a slave rebellion and help take this city for our King. This Moor, Alicax, was trustworthy, but unlucky. He was caught outside the gates of Orán, brought back, judged and impaled on a stake. Again, in front of my eyes, another execution, that stick scrounging inside him sluggishly, up and up and up until he bled to death. It took twenty-four hours. Again, a friend who refused to implicate me. And again, Hassan stood in judgment over me.

How to talk my way out of this one? The letter was in my handwriting, flourished my signature, proposed a slave rebellion. I told the supreme sovereign of all Algiers that the letter was part of a play I was composing for the prisoners, empty words meant for the stage. But Alicax, so gullible that he had believed I was able to dispense a dukedom to him, thought that delivering the false letter to real people would reap rewards for him, an island or a peninsula at least. The poor man was deluded, I said to Hassan. Is that my fault, the madness of others? Hassan was amused by the sheer audacity of my excuse, that I would think he was as naïve as that simpleminded Alicax. But I will spare you, Christian, he said. If I cut out that tongue of yours, cut off the head that will no longer be yours, I'd do myself a disservice, lose a buffoon and gain boredom. Cast this Cervantes in chains for another five months, not that I think this, or anything else, will teach him not to conspire. He was right. It was not long before I was attempting one last escape, the fourth one.

1579. I convinced Onofre Exarque, a merchant from Valencia to buy a boat for a large group I had organized. All was ready, we were to embark that very night and once more we were betrayed, this time by a defrocked priest whose name I choose not to remember. I went into hiding but when Hassan announced the execution of anyone who sheltered me, I gave myself up. Here we were once more, the master of Algiers and his lowliest subject, here was I once more, as in the cave episode, taking all the blame, sparing the others in the plot. And here was I, speechless this time, saved by the intercession of the Holy Virgin.

Or maybe more worldly matters weighed in. Hassan had just been recalled to Constantinople by the Sultan and craved to collect all the money he could for his voyage. But Fray Juan Gil, who had come from Spain to ransom as many prisoners as possible, did not have the thousand escudos Hassan insisted I was worth, not even close to that sum. Hassan had me dragged into his presence: Alright, Cervantes, you're coming with me on my voyage home, let's see if your family loosens its purse strings once they realize the tremendous trouble you're in. And indeed there I found myself *on the last day of Hassan's rule, in the galleys of his ship, chained to the oars, painfully aware that I would never come back from the Sultan's city on the Bosporus if my owner sailed off with me and his other hostages and the riches he had stolen from the people of Algiers who were dying of famine and plague in the streets, you could hear their bodies as they fell, as they cried out for help. I was almost as despairing as those poor souls, oblivious to the fact that Hassan had lowered my ransom price by half, and that Fray Juan Gil was scrambling right then and there to obtain the money from some charitable soul, I would have been doomed if at the very last minute that holy priest had not shown up to set me free. Free to return to this sweet and virtuous welcome you gentlemen have afforded me, so full of Christian piety and compassion. With one more task ahead of me.*

And at that point Cervantes dipped his good hand into the bag he carried and fished out the bundle of letters, which back then were freshly crisp and recently penned and expecting swift delivery, that's how he ended his story as he thrust them into the faces and under the nostrils of these men who had spoiled his homecoming.

These are letters, gentlemen, that I wrote for each of the cautivos left behind in Algiers, those I sought out one by one, personally, while I waited for the boat that would bring me here to Valencia, to you and your kind and tender embrace. The men nobody would pay a maravedí *for, the ones who will die over there without seeing their families or friends and certainly not people like you, the ones who will never be rescued. I would already be on my way to reading those words to these* destinatarios *if I had not been so opportunely intercepted by your worships. So, you have done what you call your duty. It is time that I did mine. Now then.*

Did you get every word of this, did your notary, this Carrasco, write it all down? Do you want to read it back to me so I can sign my name, so you can say now you know, now all Spain will know why I have nothing to be ashamed of, how Miguel de Cervantes— and Cortinas!—managed, how I managed to survive!

That's what he said, a breathless diatribe, a dramatic opening of the *cortinas* sounding so true and passionate and compelling that they could not but applaud him, all three men, even the notary Carrasco who was supposed to be neutral, merely note down the defendant's every term, that recital from the thirty-three-year-old Miguel elicited their bravos, their amazement and contrition and awe.

Though I agreed that such enthusiasm was justified, I still was wary of these men. If I had been them I would have harbored malicious, irate, maybe vengeful thoughts—he had, after all, insulted and humiliated them. But they seemed sincere, suggested—were they being sarcastic?—that given his particular aptitude for the theatre, his literary career should be dedicated to writing *comedias* about life in Algiers, entertain and by doing so educate the boisterous audience of the *corrales* about what it meant to be captive in that Moorish city of sin and piracy, persuade the theatre patrons to vacate their pockets of money better destined to ransom hostages and demand that the King arm an expedition to recover all of North Africa for Christendom, "let your fellow countrymen understand, through imaginary characters, the plight of those abandoned, all those who died without hope." Indeed, the three men, Marín and Garrido and the notary Carrasco, had been sufficiently impressed with Miguel's ardor and gallantry to recommend him for a mission to Orán, a chance to revisit those pitiless lands as a spy for the King. They begged his pardon for doubting his blood heritage and making lewd, absurd, nasty insinuations, they hadn't meant any of them, not one of the shameful questions and provocations, "please forgive us but what other way of pressing and vetting you, of making sure you are indeed the man for the mission?"

And then, to my astonishment, Miguel de Cervantes accepted that offer to return to the very Barbary Coast he had just fled from. Without seeming to care that, if he was again enslaved, this time nobody would rescue him. Not his impoverished and insolvent family that no longer had the means, and certainly not the debtors who had loaned the money and would never risk more capital for a man so rash as to blindly and stubbornly traipse back into the lion's den. Without seeming to care, still worse, that if he was recaptured in Algiers, I would end up being swallowed up, along with him, by the jaws of Islam and the Arabic tongue, deprived of the language and air of Spain that we both needed to give expression and birth to my adventures, the language and air that had beckoned me into being.

Confronted by this threat to his safety—and mine—I was overcome with dread, so alarmed that I dared to send him an urgent and official message, the first of many, I couldn't help myself, was unable to rein in my impetuousness, gave him advice he did not seek and would not have heeded had he heard it.

Because he was holding close to his chest a secret reason why he was so adamant to set out on that insensate voyage. If Marín and Garrido and the notary Carrasco had guessed what that reason was, what he was hiding beneath the role he was playing to such perfection, the true face behind the mask and supposedly open curtains he presented, they would have aborted that mission and forbidden him to travel. As for me, my influence on his soul was insignificant, even if I had been able to guess why he was willing to impulsively expose himself to such dangers. In any case, I did not know, at that point, as those three interrogators never would, that someone was waiting for him in Algiers, someone whose name and existence Miguel had abstained from revealing.

Only when Martín de Córdoba, the governor of Orán, had arranged for Miguel to be smuggled back into Algiers to gather information, did I understand what urgent fierce body had compelled him to undertake that assignment. Only after Cervantes, disguised under Arab robes, had been brought by Walid, the Berber spy who was our guide, to the accommodations of a merchant from Constantinople who, in exchange for a bagful of gold, disclosed to Cervantes that there was no danger, in fact, of an imminent attack on Spanish coasts, as the Great Turk's main preoccupation was the Persian Empire to the Far East, only once Cervantes had noted the movements and intentions of the enemy fleet and the corsairs, and was done with that part of his task and taken in the waning Mediterranean light to a palace just off the Street of the Great Souk, only when he snuck in through a back entrance, only then, only then . . .

Only then did I learn of the existence of the woman he loved, the woman who had saved his life, and that he hoped to convince to come back with him to Spain, only then, on that June 4th, 1581—it was Corpus Christi—did I meet Zahara.

THREE

" . . . For a knight errant without love is like a tree without leaves or fruit, like a body without a soul."

—*Don Quixote de la Mancha*

HE TOUCHED HER hand. Before she had the chance to unveil her face in the flickering darkness of that room in her husband's palace in Algiers, before they exchanged a word, his hand reached out to her hand, as if to verify that she was not a phantom or an apparition.

She was most definitely not.

Her devastating sensuality opened a door inside Cervantes, broke it open so wide and brazenly that I was able to tumble through it, start feeling for the first time what he was feeling, when he touched her I was also touching her, for the first time I was plunged inside his body and not a bystander, not merely looking on as he fingered and stroked and caressed her hand as if it was the world incarnate.

Zahara performed that miracle for me.

I was struck instantaneously by the softness of her skin, its creaminess, the supple invitation of the fingers, the promise emanating from the palm and mount of Venus, I was in awe of the blood pulsing inside her like a quiet raging stream, spellbound by the sheer reality of the flesh, the flesh, and caverns inside caverns calling to be filled, that dusky, shuddering sanctuary. And the perfume swirling from her every pore, rose petals and salvia, rosemary and fine oil and leaves from orange trees and perhaps a whiff of pomegranate extract, enough to make me giddy, enough to make Cervantes murmur, "The same soap, the same soap, Zahara, you are still making your soap, oh I could find you in a crowd if I were blind."

"But you are not blind, my love."

And then Miguel lifted her veil, looked deep into her eyes, and then closed his and their lips found each other, her breath in his throat, his legs trembling, her slight moan, and I . . . I felt the need to recoil.

In terror.

Due to the realization. That I was terrified of her. Not just of her. Frightened of any woman, fearful of every body of any and every and whichever female on this earth that lives or has ever lived.

When I was brought into the world that afternoon on the Valencia beach, I was, like any recently arrived creature on this earth, entirely ignorant about even a vestige of the erotic. To the point that the aberrant hints regarding passion and perversity dropped by those men during Miguel's interrogation hardly registered at the time. Nor did Cervantes himself do anything in the months that followed, to help illuminate me about sex, almost went out of his way, it could be said, to keep my virginal innocence intact.

Because Miguel never attempted the slightest amorous adventure upon his return to Spain. Nothing of the sort. Apart from fidgeting away some time with his mother and sisters, visiting an aunt at a convent, Miguel steered clear of women. No prostitutes, no jabs at seducing a pretty vixen, no flirting in the taverns, no hankering after lasses in the streets, nothing. To the point that his very avoidance or aversion of any female magnetism went entirely unremarked by me, only became clear in retrospect, when those fingers of his entwined those fingers of Zahara's.

That's how guileless I was, a neophyte, back when I started my journey, so different than I am now, eighteen years later, an avid voyeur in this Sevilla jail, now that I have, as time passed, witnessed many a tumultuous bed turned upside down and sheet turned inside out by my Miguel and listened to a myriad of dirty, double-edged jokes and can distinguish the scent of semen from the aura of female cavities. If I was acquainted with the opposite sex at all during those inaugural months of my coexistence with Miguel, before his meeting with Zahara flung open my eyes and my senses, it was through a book of chivalry that he had been re-reading since his arrival in Spain. Almost the first thing he had done, gladdening me, was to purchase it, a fat volume featuring the first part of the life and exploits of the invincible Don Belianís de Grecia, the greatest knight of all time. The protagonist's pursuit of the Princess Florisbella of Persia, the most beautiful woman in the world, filled me with honorable amazement and immaculate longing, and the aspiration to save her from evil sorcerers and undeserving suitors. I learned from that remote heroine that ladies should be adored as extraordinary creatures from an unearthly realm, superior in virtue to any mortal man, lovely and clean as the clearest sky and a balm to the birds themselves, but without question unstained by any human desire or animal inclinations. In the book there had been no mention of hot lips, or of a tongue entangled in another tongue, no reference to a masculine hand ascending around the contours of a breast, no frantic squeezing back on behalf of the female partner. No, what he and she were doing was not right, this was not what the novel had pristinely described, what I had read peering blissfully over the selfsame shoulder of Miguel to which this Zahara wench was now clinging, I could feel her fingernails digging into his back, trailing carnally downwards towards—

Suddenly, she pushed him away. Their bodies were separating, a blessed space had begun to yawn between them.

For a few moments, none of us spoke, not Miguel, not Zahara, certainly not me, alert to what might happen next, my heart beating madly, the humors in my body boiling—not because of lust, no, I wanted nothing to do with that uncomfortable yearning for somebody else's intimate vastness, no, what was flooding me was something I had not yet felt, never expected to feel, hardly knew how to name.

I was jealous.

What right did she have to fondle him in that way, to greet him in that way, to have thoroughly explored him in a manner I did not wish to even imagine? He was mine, Cervantes belonged to me, had been born for me to ride and hide inside and rise or fall with.

And he had come here, Miguel had journeyed to Algiers to rescue her as if she were the Princess Florisbella in a magic castle, induce her to come back with him to Spain. That insight hit me like the compact, waving arms of a giant, knocked the breath out of me. Those other women in his life, mother and sisters and the prioress aunt, they were no threat to my prospects. This Zahara temptress was another matter. He was ready to risk his life—and mine, though he did not know it—in order to see her once more. And might be willing to stay in Algiers—how could he refuse the incitement of the abyss inside her?—if she rejected his offer to escape. Had she rejected that offer? Or had that woman broken out of their embrace, separated herself, for another reason? Was she afraid of something, somebody else?

As if Cervantes could read my mind:

"Your husband? You're scared he . . ."

"He's away. Off Livorno, this time, with his five ships. Swifter than the ones he had before—with tall sails now. Looking for booty. And Christians who may bring an attractive ransom."

"Like me."

"Like you."

"Did you share his bed before he left? Kiss him before he left? Asked him please, this time, my love, my husband, father of my only child, this time please don't cut off the arm of one of the galley slaves, don't use the stump to beat the oarsmen into a frenzy. Did he kiss you and promise to be good?"

"He doesn't need oarsmen anymore. I told you. Tall sails."

"So you'll kiss him, kiss him and more, when he gets back. As long as he lets you pray secretly to the Virgin, save some poor bastard from being executed—"

"As I did with you, as he did with you, not once, many times—"

"And each time you paid him with your body, the body that I—"

"You think it was easy? To say darling to him? And yet, 'Darling,' I said, 'my Spanish friend, the captive who entertains me and so many others in the patio with his plays, darling, he's in trouble again.' 'What? Again?' 'Yes, he's high-spirited, he loves liberty, like you do, husband, is that a sin? Could you help him?' I pleaded with him. 'Would you, dear husband?'

And not only that. He even let me go and tend to you when you were sick and dying in that horrible hospital—"

"You should have let me die there. Because these months without you, they've been—it's as if I were dead. And I will be dead, I will die, Zahara, if you don't come back with me now. Listen well to what I'm saying: without your love, I'm lost."

"The things men say! I'm dead without you. Lost without you. You know what I've learned? We mortals die of many ills, but not of love. You will survive and so will I."

"Your body, maybe, but your soul? What does it do to you daily, to live among these men, the pirates who killed your father, cast him unblessed into those waters, without even a chance to confess, how can you smile at them when you pass them in the street?"

"Don't, Miguel, don't make this any harder than—"

"Pass them on the street and smile at them," Cervantes insisted, as she began to shake and tremble, "beasts who made slaves of you and your mother, how can you stand living among them, today and tomorrow and forever, day after day, hour after hour?"

I had been trying to absorb all this new information. So, she had been a slave as well? Someone powerful in Algiers had fallen in love with her, she had traded on that love, used it to save Cervantes, they had met in a courtyard—he had mentioned to the interrogators something about small plays he put on—and he and Zahara had become . . .—what had they become, when, how? there was so much I did not understand. I was transfixed, furiously trying to make sense of what I was being forced to behold.

So much passion!

Because Miguel took her in his arms again, almost violently.

"That smell," he said, breathing in the black cascade of her hair. "Always, always, that smell of your soap. Come back, come back with me, let me smell your skin till the day I die." He paused, as if savoring the moment. Then: "Do you know the first thing we'll do in Spain? Visit the town where you were born, where your father lived almost all his life, where your mother was never able to return?"

Zahara, for a second time, freed herself from his embrace.

"Do you remember what you used to say?" she asked. "There's a remedy for all things, save death, that's what you used to say. And you're alive. Isn't that enough? That you get to see me once more, that I get to see you one last time. And also, also I have something to show you. Come."

She took his hand and led him down a corridor. At the end of it, a eunuch dwarf stood by a door. He bowed to her, indicated that we should follow him into a room.

It was hard to discern anything in that semidarkness. Only somebody breathing delicately, only the soft cradling of lungs of someone small nearby.

The eunuch lit a candle, vanished into the shadows, we heard the door open and then close behind him.

A child was sleeping in a tiny bed.

"Your son?" Miguel whispered.

"My son?" she murmured back. "Jamaal wouldn't be sleeping in the servant's quarters. You know how well he's guarded, more strictly than when we—Silly man. Can't you tell a boy from a girl?"

"A girl? So you found her! What's her name?"

"Cristina."

"You're bringing her up as ..."

"In our faith, on the sly, just as my mother did with me. I'm sure it's what her own mother would have wanted someone like me to do."

He reached a hand out to tuft the little girl's hair back from her forehead.

Zahara stopped him.

Giving him leave to breathe deeply with the child, in unison, as if they were one creature.

"In Spain," Cervantes said, his voice almost breaking with emotion, with affection, "she could worship Jesus and His Mother freely. As could you. And your son. Oh, Lord. Aren't you tired of this double life? Islamic by day, Catholic by night, Arabic for the public world, Spanish for your dreams and for me? Don't you want to be whole, not divided against yourself?"

Abruptly, from somewhere inside the palace a sound slapped them. Someone had called out, a man's gruff voice in Arabic, another voice responding like a cutlass in the night. Zahara moved her head in the direction of the door, they should depart.

Outside, in the corridor, the dwarf had disappeared. They waited. I listened along with them. Nothing, not even an echo of an echo. The danger seemed to have passed.

"She's sweet, isn't she?" Zahara whispered. "Just like her dead father, poor man."

"At least the child is cared for. At least one promise that you kept."

"That's not fair. I always keep my promises."

"Not always."

"The cave, the cave, that stupid cave, that stupid plan to escape, I knew it was bound to fail. If I had come with you, if the renegade had learned of my participation, then who would have saved you? Oh, you are the most stubborn man I have ever—and here you are, stubborn as always."

"At least I got to see that little girl. How did you find her?"

"It took me forever. Once I discovered who owned her, and her master got wind of my interest, of course he kept raising the price—*oh no, this little slave is the favorite of my wife, my daughter, my sister, my aunt, my own favorite, so very sorry, she's priceless, beyond monetary value, how could we be separated from such a precious creature, I can't wait till she grows a bit, for her breasts and other things to bloom*—until finally, my husband sent him a threat, sell us the girl or I'll be selling your balls in the marketplace—you can see that he's not the fiend you make him out to be—and Cristina's master capitulated."

"So the girl . . .?" Miguel said. "When are you going to tell her about her father?"

"She's too young now. I don't want her to feel sad, like me when I was her age, full of anger. I know what it's like to grow up among the men responsible for a father's death . . ."

Miguel saw an opening, went on the attack again, his voice unsteady, agitated.

"And you don't want to spare her that experience? Or save Jamaal, before he gets contaminated?"

"It's impossible to get Jamaal out from—"

"I can still fight, I can rescue him, I can—"

"Offer him what? Offer her? Offer me . . . what?"

"A community, that's what I can offer. Waiting for you."

She looked deep into his eyes. She did not see me inside him, expectant, suspicious. What she saw was something else, a sort of lake of grief.

"So it was not what you expected. Your freedom."

"Better than I expected. You can't understand until you've breathed the air where you were born, the glory of hearing only the language of your parents, no enemies around you. Don't you hunger for that moment, to never again be a captive?"

She smiled and that corridor lit up as if the sun had begun to rise. "You were always good at lying, Miguel. But not to me, never to me. The return did not sit well with you, go well for you. Not a hero celebrated by all, no favors from the King, not the wondrous future you drew for me. How much are they paying you for this mission, huh? How many paltry *escudos*? Did anyone offer—yes, offer—to pay off your debts? The truth now, I've earned the right to hear the truth."

Cervantes said nothing. But from her shadows she could see, as I could from my own perch, that those words had pierced him, were draining him, collapsing every defense, making him ever more fragile. Unable to hide his desolation from her, just as he has never been able to hide it from me.

She should have accorded him some solace, as I would have done if I'd been given half the chance, but that was not her way, she did not relent. "I warned you: do not believe that good will come to you because you have done good. That's not how it works. *Al-jeza'l-ihsan illa'l-ihsan.*" She translates for him, unquestionably for me: "Is there any reward for goodness except the chance to do more good? From the *Surat ar-rahman*, the Chapter of Mercy."

"You don't seem to be showing much of that Koranic mercy of yours towards me. What happened to the Bible, eh? What happened to do unto others as you would have them do unto you?"

"Except they didn't, did they? They didn't respond to your goodness with goodness, but with malice. Go on, say it. They responded with malice, they betrayed you, your countrymen, they did not see you, really see you, see who you were, like I am seeing you here, now, right now. Say it."

"No."

"Say it."

"They didn't see me."

"You were going to write, Miguel, create beauty. *Ihsan. Ihsan.* Isn't it wonderful, that word, *ihsan,* extraordinary that the word for goodness in the Koran is *ihsan,* which is also beauty? Have you forgotten what I taught you, what you taught me? Tell me, tell me. Is there room under the Spanish stars for all manner of wisdom, for what we learned from each other? Tell me. Can you really, with your hand on your heart, can you really promise that Spain will welcome me when it has shown someone like you no pity? Did they interrogate you on your return? Did they? Did they?"

He mouthed the word "Yes," so dry and unobtrusive that only someone as close to him as Zahara, as close as I was, could hear it.

"So what about me? Will they ask me about every belief I have now, or have had yesterday, or may have tomorrow and the next day? Will they force me to do penance? Will they keep me in a convent for a year while they investigate? Will they accept my accent in a language that no longer feels like my own?

Will they ask me to denounce the friends I have made here, the women who come to this palace and dance and bewilder the night with their incantations and make prophecies about the future and cure my son with their herbs? Will your rulers not brand me as a witch? Can I bring the Koran with me? Tell me, tell me. Can I bring the Koran? No, they would burn that book they call cursed, idolatrous, a blasphemy, burn the word *ihsan*. And then burn me. Or must I hide as I have to hide here? Will I ever belong anywhere, Miguel? No, I'll be a stranger forever. Like you, except you won't admit it, you prefer to lie to yourself, always full of illusions. Why should I not read the Koran in Spain and read the Bible in Algiers? While that's not possible, I'd rather stay here. At least I'll be safe, can protect my son, protect that girl."

And that's when I let my guard down, realized she was not a threat to me or to Miguel, when I understood she would never return with us, that it did not matter if she was Christian or Muslim or both or neither, that she, in spite of the storm of certitudes with which she dazzled us both, in spite of her outbursts of fury, was as lost as any child born in our times or any other century, that's when I started to love her.

Before our journey to Algiers, I would have thought it was madness for anyone to wish to stay in a land of heretics, not jump at the possibility of making public profession of her faith and serving the God who died on the Cross. The idea I had of that city came from what Miguel had described to those three men in Valencia: the mouth of Hell, full of demons and pestilential streets and martyrs being tortured. But my experience a few months later differed surprisingly from that account. Once we crossed the desert from Orán and drew in sight of

Algiers in the distance, I was greeted by orchards filled with fruit amidst fields of green, crystal clear streams flowing into fresh fountains, hills gleaming with spinach and beanstalks. And gardens! Miguel was offered peaches by the laborers under the hot sun and the juice dribbled down onto his bearded chin and then his eyes lifted and there, on the horizon, was the city where he had been held captive, bright with towers and casements, the domes of mosques and a grandiose citadel beckoning from within those immense fortifications. And soon enough our Berber scout, Walid, was guiding Cervantes across the moat of Àrab Ahmed and elbowing his way past merchants and janissaries milling near the Gate of Bab al-Wad and I was hit by the enchantment of the bustle and the life and, oh, the spices wafting into me. Nor was I alone in that moment of sheer sensual bliss. My Miguel was taking it all in with gulping mouthfuls, as if he were drinking the air rather than breathing it, already savoring the succulent couscous, what the scent of chickpeas and lamb searing on sticks augured simultaneously, and such a riot and glorious chaos of colors and clothes that our eyes hurt, kaftans and vests and robes and veils and turbans, and houses so white, so clean, so calm, that they brought peace to our fearful hearts. And all those shops and artisans, makers of saddles and scimitars, and the barbers and basket weavers and tanners and tailors, and everybody talking and calling out, a chorus of voices in all languages imaginable coming from bodies of every shade of skin and every nation in the Mediterranean and beyond, and the sea, the sea, bursting blue with vessels.

It was difficult to believe that without slaves the city would crumble and cease to function, that it contained suffering and blood and torment, easy to forget that so many captives seethed inside dungeons and on its fields and quarries, or that Cervantes had been chained to walls and condemned to death and watched his friends being executed. The city seemed impervious to those memories, and Zahara had found a way to live without thinking about this constantly, without dwelling on the murder of her own father—where? how? why? None of that was clear when she first crossed my path, and I have been unable since then to plumb the mystery of her identity. All I nurse is the rubble of that two-hour conversation, those lips that still burn in my memory, that fire with which she challenged Miguel, that sorrow she endured and tried not to show and could not erase, all I am left with is an unfinished, perpetually fluid story, that enigma.

Where had she been born? Brought up? How had she ever found herself—a girl captured on the high seas, with a father slaughtered and a mother enslaved—in a position to save Cervantes, not once but at least twice? What sort of bizarre pact had she entertained with this husband, so differently described by one and the other, as a brute or an angel, that he intervened to spare a prisoner who kept trying to escape? Can women be so powerful? And who was this girl Cristina? Was her father really dead? Could it be that Cervantes was secretly her father and neither he nor Zahara wanted to acknowledge that relationship, perhaps the death they spoke of was a metaphor, of the sort that writers love, death as departure, death as separation, did they define it as a form and foreboding of death that the child should never know the man who had made her inside a woman? And what woman? Where? How? Why?

Questions that have remained unanswered in these intervening years, that I still have not resolved here in the Sevilla jail. Because as soon as Miguel left Zahara's presence, it was like she no longer existed. He did not mention her, not once, not to his family, not to his dearest friends, not to anybody—just as he had omitted that love affair from the tale of captivity he told the three insolent men. Each time I tried to probe her presence, slowly and selectively, careful not to be intrusive, he automatically, inevitably, instantaneously, barred my way. He had shut that segment of himself inside ramparts higher and thicker and more impregnable than the ones that had confined him in Algiers, a room where he kept her captive. A captive of his mind, a captive of his heart, close to her though their bodies might be separated forever.

It was what she had told him to do, when they finally said goodbye.

"My body remains here, Miguel, but my mind, my heart, my words, go with you, that's something nobody can ever take away from you. And faith. Don't let them take from you the faith I have in who you are, the faith in yourself that you must never lose, no matter what. Because what you survived here was easy compared to what is coming."

Her hand reached out to his neck and then to his beard and back to the neck and up the head to his hair and she drew him to her and then, again, the warm supple lips of eternity, and then:

"So I need you to remember this."

"As if I could ever forget your lips."

"No. Not my lips. This. Remember what I am about to say. You who are sad because of those who died in your stead, because you cannot bring back the dead, remember this when you are tempted by bitterness, remember this: be sure those who died, those who were left behind, did not suffer in vain. Be sure you make something, something valuable, of the life that has been given to you."

"Without you? What can I do without you by my side?"

She responded with the one word I had been hoping to hear, she said the one word that transformed her into an ally on my road to enlightenment.

"Write," she whispered to him—and did not need to add what she and he must have been thinking, *because when you write verses they will be about me, and when you write plays they will be about your captivity and my Algiers, and if you write that pastoral novel you've been sketching out for years in your head, it will someday reach these shores and I will read it and read you and read myself into every female character and every sigh and then it will be true that I will never forget you and you will never forget me. And when the time comes for your masterpiece, it will be a homage to life, the life I gave you and the life you gave me and will give to the whole world, a book full of people like you and me.*

Her farewell gift to him.

That one word, *write*, the one commandment he carried, along with me and her memory, back to Spain, again back to Spain, disposed to obey her.

Stories, he was bursting with stories, born of his exile and its rupture and loss, stories can be your home when everything else has been broken, I suggested to him on the ship we sailed back on, and added when we sighted the coast of Spain, I am here if you need a foundation for your wounded identity, I am here to accompany you on this adventure, not just me but others of my kind—here, nebulously close by, I could feel them awaiting their own commencement from within a darkness they shared with me, praying, as I was, for deliverance—all Miguel de Cervantes had to do was find the courage to reach out to me, to us.

But nothing turned out as I had dreamt it.

He returned from Orán and did not, just as she had presaged, receive any reward or respect. The squalid fifty *escudos* he had been paid before departing for North Africa were supplemented by fifty more, but they did not renew his contract as a spy, nor his back pay for years of soldiering in Italy, Lepanto and Tunisia. He journeyed to Lisbon where Felipe II, bent on dominating the Atlantic, had taken up residence but Cervantes never managed to meet his monarch, nor finagle the post he was seeking in the Indies. He decided to head for Madrid. As advancement through his services in war seemed ever farther away, he would try his luck, following Zahara's commands, in the world of letters, hoping that such an exercise would bring him fame and fortune. Neither of the two were to be his. He spawned—I wondered if he was taking into account the advice of Marín, Garrido and Carrasco—play after play, that were successful only insomuch as the spectators did not throw rotten lettuce at the actors, but that was it, nobody demanded that his *comedias* be performed again, he earned scarcely more than the paper and ink and *pluma* disbursed to scratch and push those words into the world. He stopped writing for the theatre. Not sure what pained him more, the audience's rebuff of his work, or its general indifference to the themes of captivity that nobody cared to see on stage—or anywhere else, for that matter—the tribulations of the Christian slaves of Algiers, not even when he reunited his male and female protagonists in a rapturously happy ending, entirely absent from his own disastrous saga.

A novel, a novel, I grumbled to him, and that is what he turned to next, though not what I desired from him: he plunged into the pastoral world, courtly youths snubbed by remote shepherdesses amid babbling streams and quiet green pastures. He considered his *Galatea* better than any other novel of that genre ever written, but besides some faint praise from wayward friends, it had not done well, did not come near to rivaling the astonishing reception of Montemayor's *La Diana*. Nor did his poems garner him more than third place in fourth rate competitions, futile exercises in vanity that I did not like, found neither inspired or inspiring, but then I had my own petty reasons to be prejudiced in favor of prose. So, everywhere, dejection and rejection—except from Anna Franca, she had really loved him, offered real support, and not once as he wooed and seduced and bedded her had my Miguel stopped thinking of Zahara. At least that is what I presumed. Otherwise why did he respond to Anna's devotion by abandoning her, pregnant and about to give birth, for a woman he cared for even less?

In effect, a few months later, at the very same time that Anna was nursing the illegitimate daughter she'd had with Cervantes, he was in a church in La Mancha, marrying Catalina de Salazar.

I'm ashamed to admit that I approved of his choice: I believed, as my host did, that she possessed lands and houses and vineyards in Esquivias, we both assumed that, with her assets at his disposal, he could settle down in that small town in La Mancha, what better place than La Mancha indeed to spend the rest of his life following Zahara's exhortation to write. I initially felt it was justified—writers must be ruthless in some things!—that he should exaggerate his own prospects, dupe her into that engagement by proclaiming that he was about to be elevated by the King to some plum job.

Not that he stopped dreaming of Zahara, and as to his wife . . .—well, I couldn't even begin to guess what her inner thoughts might be, but I suppose Catalina, who didn't even know how to sign her own name to the marriage contract, fell in love with both the illusion of grandeur he projected and the quite real allure he exuded.

This will not last, I said to myself, muttered to him on the wedding night and through the loveless nights that followed. You've fooled each other and thus will deserve—a conclusion I came to reluctantly—the mutual loneliness you have condemned yourselves to.

And sure enough, belatedly discovering that he could not live off her nonexistent *rentas*, nor write a lasting word in that dull company, where only the local barber and the resident priest had ever perused a book, he had absconded for many years to Andalucía as the King's Commissioner. It had been easier to sway Hassan Pasha in that Algiers palace than avaricious monks and wary merchants and famished peasants in Spain, yet sway them he did, town by town, and swayed as well on mules until his aching back cried out to stay and stop, and on and on he strayed, from *pueblo* to *pueblo* and *venta* to *venta*, wandering as his bumbling father had many decades ago, with the same dust from the same roads dismaying Miguel's lungs and decaying his eyes, and I did not sway or weigh at all in his mind, not even as a plodding rhyme, not at all. Not a word written, not a verse, just numbers and reports and complaints and defenses against false accusations and explanations of why there was no surplus of stocks and an excess of recalcitrance on the part of the subjects of His Majesty, worse still when the Invincible Armada floundered and he was forced to change jobs and start collecting taxes and arrears, and all for what? So that over a decade later he could have less coins at his command when his travels were completed than when they had started, all so he could end up here in this abysmal prison in Sevilla, jailed for a debt that he did not owe, accused of stealing money he had deposited with a banker who had disappeared, all so that eighteen years after Marín and Garrido and Carrasco had applauded him and augured a bright future, here they are again, witnesses of his failure to carry out even one of his aspirations to fame and magnificence and recognition.

To add insult to injury, they had not aged like him, looking exactly the same as when he had last suffered their contempt in Valencia. As if they had been drinking daily from a fountain of youth and pride. As if time had not passed for them. But for him, for him, not only time had passed, life had also passed, passed him by.

Mocked by Zahara's last words of encouragement and faith, words that only I continued to believe in, that he should make something, something valuable, of the life the dead had given him. Abandoned by everyone but me. Maimed not by the Turks at a glorious naval battle but by his own self-inflicted insignificance. Nobody to blame but himself. Irrelevant.

Not a writer. A scribbler.

Not knowing that, for now, scribbling is exactly what he needs.

FOUR

"From all that you have told me, dearest brothers, it is clear to me that though you have been punished for your faults, the hardships you are about to suffer are not to your liking, and you go towards them against your will and free choice; and it might be that the lack of valor this one showed under torture, that this other one did not have enough money for bribes, that another one was not favored by someone powerful, and finally, the twisted judgement of the magistrate, were the cause of your perdition, not allowing you to receive the justice that you deserved. All of which I picture now in my memory in such a way that it tells me, persuades me and even forces me to display to you gentlemen the reason why heaven cast me into the world and made me profess the order of chivalry, and the vow I took to favor the disadvantaged and those oppressed by the high and mighty . . . . It seems harsh to make slaves of those whom God and Nature made free."

—*Don Quixote de la Mancha*

THIS DECISIVE DAY when those three men from his past, Marín and Garrido and Carrasco, catapult phantasmagorically back into his life, has started like every day since we arrived in the Cárcel de Sevilla.

As always, Cervantes walks to the rickety table he rents at an outrageous price from Papa Pasamonte. It is set up at one corner of this cavernous hall, next to the fruit stand attended to by a hunchback who is the brother-in-law of one of the guards, and who greets Cervantes effusively each morning, seeing in his mutilated hand a sign of their membership in the same exclusive club of the crippled. Cervantes nods at him companionably and arranges the foolscap of papers in an orderly row, his fingers numb from the cold, trying to be oblivious to the murmurs of an old crone who, a foot or two away on a dirty rug, reads the cards to a disgraced nobleman with squinty eyes, jailed for forging letters of credit from foreign agents, in order to pay for his opulent clothes and lifestyle.

On the other side of the table, anxious, pimply, with lovely hazel eyes like recently made honey, is Álvaro Ponce, a cocky youngster known as *Cortadillo* because of the stealth and celerity with which he steals purses. The lad has been assured by Pasamonte that Miguel de Cervantes, for a few *reales*, will get the mother Álvaro has not laid eyes on in five years—nor even attempted to contact—to forgive him, send him the money from Cádiz that he requires to survive this confinement, perhaps even bail him out before he is condemned to the galleys for sixteen years.

"Here, Álvaro, is what I have written to this saintly *madre* in your name. That you are in this prison out of love. *I loved a basket of clothes so much that I hugged it close to me, and it would not let me go, nor could I have scorned its round full belly smelling of what was recently and freshly washed, reminding me of when I lodged inside you all those months.*"

"You don't know my mother. She'll be doubly angry that, instead of repenting, I am making light of these sins."

"She will be glad that you are breaking the news to her like this, with a joke. Her smile will ready her for the rest of the letter, brimming with endearments and a sonnet invoking the

Mother of God and her mercy. And, at the end, as if you had just come to the idea, a plea for help."

"But she knows I'm no poet, that I can't write my own name."

"Mothers only want a pretext, flimsy as it may be, to think the best of their progeny. She'll see this letter as proof that the academy you went to these five years has not been an academy of crime but of elegant letters. I'll add that in, how you have been schooled by your experiences. And jail made you surpass yourself."

"I have only been here two days."

"How long does it take for a miracle to bless us? An hour, a minute, the flash of a second. And people believe what they need in order to get through the night. Leave it to me. I will convince her you are here only due to lack of grease."

"Right! I get it. I could not grease the palms of the *corchetes* who detained me, didn't grease the wheels of justice so the magistrate would arrest someone else."

"Right indeed! You lacked the grease of money which is what we will finally squeeze out of the woman who gave you birth to bribe the right lawyer and *oidor*. Would that my mother were still alive, so she could rescue me from this penitential fortress, as she did when I was in Algiers. But if I were not here, then I would not be able to rescue you, would I? Let's drink, then, to my misfortune."

I like this Miguel more than the solemn, serious, sad one. He switches from one Miguel to the other rapidly, as if there were two people inside him, two masks he imposes on his face. So, I am not surprised when his mood abruptly changes as soon as he glimpses, as I do, those three men entering the hall as if they owned it, taking possession of the air and the noise and the inmates merely by the way they swagger in, ensuring that everyone realizes who they are and what they can do, ensuring that Cervantes knows they are headed his way. Which makes my prideful Miguel, still smarting from their first encounter, even more determined to pay them no heed.

"Good luck then," Cervantes says to Álvaro, studiously avoiding the sight of those men advancing towards him, "to both of us."

"Thank you, Don Miguel."

"Thank Papa Pasamonte, who has decided you are worthy of trust and that you will soon have the *reales* from your devout mother to pay for this letter and, if I have been eloquent enough, your own liberation."

Álvaro is leaving, bowing, and scraping, and Constanza Salvadora, the next client, is already approaching the table, when Cervantes adds, loud enough for everyone to hear, definitely a message for those men, that he is not entirely defenseless, that he has held onto his dignity in this most bereft of places, that he will not let them demean him, not now, not ever again.

"And don't call me 'Don.' Such a title has not been bestowed on me and I am sure it never will. I am the son of myself and what I have done, and nobody and nothing else. *Cada uno es hijo de sus obras.*"

There it is, that phrase, those words that thrill my old heart, constitute an unmistakable step in my direction. But before I can congratulate him, embolden him to persist and store words like these, *every man is the son of his own works,* in some recess of his brain for a better day that perhaps, *quién sabe,* will be today, yes, yes, I almost dare to predict, as I invariably do each morning, that this will be the day, before I have the time to bolster Cervantes with an encouraging message of my own, those three intruders beat me to it and spring into action.

They shove the imposing woman standing in line to one side, cut in front of Constanza Salvadora who, despite the lethal ticking of the clock of her life, has been patiently waiting to be attended to, Marín treats this supplicant desperate to receive assistance from her Knight of Shining Words as if she were a slab of meat swinging from a hook in a butcher shop.

Cervantes sees the woman reach into a pocket of her skirt where he knows that she carries a long razor blade, and in order to stop her from taking a step forward to punish these strangers who have usurped her place without so much as an excuse me, thank you, would you mind, in order to make sure she won't exact on their faces a token of her trampled dignity, my Miguel nods his head imperceptibly, warns her off, he will take care of this impudence in his own good time and way.

She smiles, fingers her razor surreptitiously, ready to leap into action. Too often has she crossed paths with such scum and knows, as I do, the harm they can do to her friend Cervantes.

They show, however, no sign whatsoever of hostility. Their tone is disarming and cordial.

"What a pity, Miguel, to see you in these dire straits."

"My friend, did we not tell you to stay out of trouble?"

"Miguel, Miguel, didn't we specify that? Didn't Carrasco here note our *advertencia* down in his report? But we come not to scold you, surely you know how well disposed we are towards your person."

"As soon as we heard of the indictment, we said, wait a second, we know this Miguel, we even recommended him for a secret mission—wait a second, we said, he would never have done anything like that . . ."

"There must be some sort of misunderstanding, we said, we went to Gaspar de Vallejo, this magistrate who's prosecuting you, we've been close with him for years—"

"And the truth is that he's not very good at his job, keeps making mistakes, truth is he doesn't know how to add two plus two, thinks it's three or five. Made a mess of your case. We pointed out that you couldn't possibly owe 2,557,029 *maravadíes*, that those taxes were collected by you and deposited with that duplicitous banker and that you are the one who is owed a large back salary, but he wouldn't budge."

"He's stubborn, this man, so we calculate it will be another four or five months before you're cleared . . . ."

"But we were able to wrench from him—it was like pulling teeth, but we're not ones to relent—that if we found you could be of service, he would consider offering you conditional release—"

"Into our custody, of course."

"As we said, a stubborn man. Like you. Though once in a while, reasonable. *You want to speak to this Cervantes? You want to help him? I won't stand in your way.*"

"And that's why we've come. Friends help friends, that's what you did in Algiers for the other captives, that's what we do here in Spain for deserving souls like you."

"So what if we find ourselves a quiet spot, no prying eyes or indecent ears, where we can propose something mutually beneficial to us all?"

That other time, back in Valencia, his strategy had been to pretend at first to cooperate only to finally, to their astonishment and my delight, swamp them with a furious torrent of words. On this occasion, he prefers to let them drone on unimpeded, until he judges that the right moment has arrived to emit a simple, unemotional instruction, terse and direct: "Gentlemen, please wait your turn in line. I must finish with my client, who has already recompensed Señor Pasamonte for my services, and, I can assure you, has more urgent business with me than yours could ever be. You suggested that I cultivate patience, as I recall. Perhaps it behooves you now to learn from the patience of these good people, given that I doubt you can imitate their integrity."

I feel a certain satisfaction at how gracefully he is embarrassing these bullies, showing them he is in charge here, in this tiny, constricted parcel of Spain, even if they own the wide and wild world out there, even if he suspects, as I do, that he will soon pay dearly for this defiance. But he will not let them interfere with his mission.

He has become, in the last few months, a wordsmith for the poor, the neglected, the discarded, the doomed, the misunderstood, the lovelorn, representing the nasty and the kind, the illiterate and the ill-advised, the justly and unjustly jailed, those who are about to die at the stake and those who will soon get out of prison and continue their life of virtue or crime. And the lonely, above all he renders service to all those who are lonely, all those who believe this Miguel de Cervantes performs miracles, a savior whose words can translate despair into hope or, at the very least, provide the delusion of comfort.

His specialty: farewell letters for those about to die.

It all began a few hours after arriving at the Cárcel de Sevilla, a vocation he discovered through Alonzo Ballesteros, his first client.

To be executed three days later—that was the sentence—in the Plaza de San Francisco—death by hanging and then his body to be quartered and his head exhibited in a cage at the top of La Puerta de Almenilla.

Cervantes had listened to his needs, his story, his exculpation, his love for his wife Amparo and their three daughters—noting it all down stone-faced, almost mechanically. As if he considered this process to be no more than a commercial transaction: Alonzo was at a loss for words, Cervantes had them in abundance, Alonzo had some coins, Cervantes had some skills. And Papa Pasamonte would protect the writer and confer prestige if he performed well, send other inmates his way.

Regarding the fees stemming from his employment, the terms were easily negotiated with Pasamonte. A writer, he explained loftily, is like a baker who adds the right amount of yeast to the dough, like a carpenter or a stonemason who builds something sturdy and useful, delivering the goods for which he was paid, and should be recompensed accordingly.

And it was with that strict professionalism that he tackled the Alonzo Ballesteros job at hand, got down to business that first night in the Cárcel de Sevilla: readying two letters for the next morrow.

He tackled the most imperative one first, directed to Teresa Clavijo, the widow of the man Alonzo had been accused of killing. If she officially forgave him there was a chance his life would be spared, he would only be given two hundred lashes and six years in the galleys. She had indicated to Padre de León, who had been acting as intermediary, her unwillingness to move a finger to help the murderer who had left her two boys fatherless. In spite of the four hundred *escudos* of compensation collected by Alonzo's comrades in the Army, the infantrymen who had marched to the drum he beat during decades of battle, the widow obdurately refused to cooperate: Alonzo had confessed to the crime and blood spilled calls for more blood.

Cervantes carefully laid out, therefore, the reasons why Alonzo was innocent: how could he have committed that offense against society and God if several witnesses placed him ten leagues away at the time of the crime, witnesses who had not been deposed by the *alguacil*, the constable who arrested him. Without directly fingering this officer, Cervantes subtly implied that he might be the real culprit, or was framing Alonzo to cover up for somebody powerful, rich enough to get away with murder. As to the confession, it was extracted from the accused under torture. At the sixth turn of the rope that was splitting his arm from the armpit, Alonzo indicated he was disposed to confess to whatever they wished. Not that this stopped the *verdugos*. They kept at it anyway, drowning him over and over again in a bucket of water, just to make sure the truth he would sputter was the one they had been paid to dig out of his throat and aching chest.

It was here that Cervantes showed his mastery of the prose he had not practiced for so long. He did his utmost to graphically place the widow inside the perspective of the tormented body of Alonzo Ballesteros, see the flesh being torn and feel the water and smell the excrement, hear the howls and maledictions. So, she could understand why the accused man had agreed to the false version his tormentors made him sign.

My only sin, Cervantes wrote for Alonzo, *is weakness. I prefer, dear lady, to die by hanging, a quick snap of the neck, rather than endure more days of the rack and the liquid in my lungs. But if you were to forswear this absolution, please know, Teresa Clavijo, that I will die blessing you and your husband and your two boys, with no rage or resentment in my heart, so that God can receive me in all my innocence and purity, without indecorous thoughts that would surely besmirch my soul and condemn it to Hell. My sole sorrow: that my death cannot bring your husband back to life, that my death does not make you any happier.*

Cervantes affixed one last touch that might move the widow to pity: Alonzo's three daughters were in danger, through no fault of their own, of losing their father as well as their honor and any chance of matrimony, as no decent man would wed a girl from a family so publicly disgraced. And he reminded her that Jesus had forgiven those who crucified him and that his mother, Mary, had tried to obtain the pardon of Judas himself, pleading that traitor's case with God the Father.

As Cervantes doubted that Teresa Clavijo would yield to these or any other entreaties, such was her desire for revenge, he had then set himself to composing the second letter. To be sent after Alonzo's execution to his wife Amparo.

I will not repeat here, my love, that I am innocent of the crime they have arrested me for. This you know all too well, as I was with you when that poor man was being murdered. If I am guilty of anything it is of not having loved you enough and now my time is done and I cannot tell you day by day what I feel and felt, what I should have told you when I had the chance. The nearness of death, however, has loosened the tongue that all my life, due to my shyness, had been unhappily constricted. Death is not shy, and murmurs words into my ears, now that I am learning what matters and what does not, now that I am free of fear and only regret so many nights spent away from you, so many hours wasted at the tavern and in the battlefields of Flanders and La Goleta, so many times I was not there to alleviate your loneliness. All that is left of me now are these words that I trust you will keep by your side, so that when your hand reaches out to the hollow that my body has left, when your fingers reach out to my absence, you will find this letter, this consolation that I write in the Cárcel Real as I await the judgment of God. As to your judgment, Amparo, may it be benevolent in the years to come, may you forgive me for this sorrow that I inflict upon you, for being so unworthy of your devotion. My eternal thanks for breathing life into me when I least warranted it. And at this point, something unforeseen happened.

Cervantes began to weep.

Alone there, in his cell, by the light of two dripping candles Papa Pasamonte had installed after banishing the other twenty-nine inmates who were supposed to sleep in those chilly quarters, sob after sob racked his body.

I was intrigued, concerned, puzzled. Of course, he felt compassion for Alonzo and his iniquitous fate, a compassion that I shared and understood. Of course, he was indignant at the injustice visited upon this innocent man, the very sort Cervantes himself was suffering in this very prison in Sevilla and that I would someday sally forth to vanquish if I ever got the chance. Of course, both he and I imagined what it would mean for Amparo to receive these syllables from a husband who was no longer alive, something tangible to hold onto as she grew old next to an empty hearth.

But none of that was enough to justify the flood of tears, the floodgate of emotion that swept over Cervantes when he finished that second letter.

He was crying for himself.

Cervantes had not been good at revealing pain. Not to his family, not to his fellow poets, not to his lover Anna Franca, or his wife Catalina Salazar—and even not to me, though nobody can claim to be closer. Strange, all these years, to be able to see from his eyes and hear with his ears and feel what he is touching, strange to *inhabit* him, and yet far too often find myself banished from the inner chambers of his intimacy, limited—as if I were not someone special—to whatever he chose to show at guarded moments if I was lucky, a curtain, yes, that *cortina* he boasted to have loosened in Valencia for those three men was generally drawn tightly shut, shrouding his thoughts, encasing them in ice.

But never, in these nearly two decades that I have accompanied him, had he been asked to write a letter saying goodbye to a loved one, or been confronted by this sort of challenge, never had he found himself groping, gasping even, for the right words to express that ultimate estrangement. There was only one way for those words to ring true, only one way for Miguel to be loyal to this man about to lose everything. Miguel's only resource: himself.

Connecting, through that letter written to Amparo in the name of Alonzo, with his own lost love, dipping into his own well of grief, he had to be thinking of Zahara in her lonely bed across the Mediterranean, hoping she was thinking of him.

But Zahara is so far, perhaps he is as dead to her as if he had been executed by Hassan Pasha, he has left her in that city of infidels without a written constellation of words to light up the dark sky of her night, to remember him by, not even a permanent goodbye such as this one that Amparo can return to, and solace herself with, during the endless years to come. *All that I will miss, that you will need and I cannot give you: to care for you when you are sick, to praise the meal you make, to share the joys of watching a daughter grow up, to cradle each other into sleep and wake when dawn and rain wash into our garden.* And now other memories came crawling through the portal of his mind, at first tentatively, then pouring forth in waves.

There it was, there it was, what he had hidden from those three men and then from everybody else and would have hidden forever from his own self if it had not been so embedded into the most intricate fabric of his memories.

There it was, the moment when Cervantes, like Alonzo now, had also faced a violent death, there it was, in front of me, inside of me as if I were living it, the occasion, that occasion, and another one when he had confronted the King of Algiers, without knowing if he was about to be beaten and hung, quartered and sliced by that master of his life and death; there was the revelation, as he wrote that letter in Sevilla, that Cervantes had once wished that he had been given the time, offered the chance, to jot down what he felt as the hours closed around him, the words he now found and used for Alonzo and his mourning and his wife.

And deeper into the slashing wound of his past I burrowed. Not just the loneliness and regret of a man who fears he is about to die began to torment him all over again. Something else, perhaps more painful, drizzled out of the hole opened by his memories.

There it was, there it was, there he was, Juan Navarra. Juan Navarra, roly and poly and smiling and able to sing like a lark ascending, stocky and short and for some reason with an eye that winked, Juan Navarra with peach juice flowing down his scraggy bit of a beard. Cervantes remembers Juan, the gardener who was tortured to death in front of his very eyes, Cervantes laments never having been able to compile for Juan a message like the one he has been writing on behalf of Alonzo. And then the figure of Alicax appears, the Moor who had remained loyal as he was impaled, somehow still believing that Cervantes would fly in like a wizard or prove to be an Emperor, and save the prisoner at the last moment, but all Cervantes can do now is watch Alicax as he dies back then and dies again in his mind, Cervantes was never able to devote to him the hours he was spending on Alonzo, leaving Cervantes alive to lament over and over again that his friends were dying then and now and forever devoid of the comfort of knowing that someone somewhere would read their last words.

And behind and inside and beneath and next to those memories, there they are, there they were, many others, Diego and Florián and Gonzalo and Hernando and so many more, the slaves who did have letters transcribed for them so someone somewhere would know something at least about their fate. Peering into his unhealed yesterdays, now that he was defenseless, now that the wall he had built around his sorrow and guilt was shattering and collapsing, a whole chorale of faces and voices and derelict lives emerged from oblivion: his fellow captives in Algiers, the ones too poor to be rescued, the ones too humble to be helped, the ones who had tried to escape and the ones who were too afraid, the ones who had labored in the fields and the mines and the households, the ones who rowed the pirate galleys on their raids and managed by some miracle not to die of exhaustion or mistreatment or thirst, the ones who had learned to work leather and wood and stone and used Cervantes as a middleman to hawk their goods at a better price, the ones who had kept the faith and saved their souls and the ones who had embraced Islam as the only way to rise in that society that did not care about lineage or pure blood, all those who would never see their home again or know if their children were growing strong and sturdy, if their sisters had succumbed to the plague, if their wives made love at night to another man, if their mother was still alive and awoke at dawn to make some hot porridge in case this was the day, this was finally the day her boy would return, all of them living on inside Miguel de Cervantes so many years later, heavier in his heart than those letters at the bottom of his bag.

Because it was true what he had boasted to Marín and Garrido and Carrasco: he had composed them himself, Cervantes had sat with each captive and written letters on their behalf that concluded, invariably, every one of them, with the same words: *I have never forgotten you. Do not forget me.*

And had consoled his ragged, desperate comrades in Algiers by swearing he would also abide by those words, that he, Cervantes, would never forget them, promising to deliver each letter personally.

It was only on his return to Spain that it began to dawn on him how difficult it would be to honor that promise. Because his debts could also, ironically, brandish those very words,

I will never forget you, it turned out that the creditors who had paid his ransom did not forget, would not forget, would remind Miguel and his mother, Miguel and his sisters, Miguel and the father who had feigned death in order to move the authorities to pity for the fraudulent widow who came begging them to help her captive child. So true that his family had not forgotten him that they now owed a fortune, they would not be allowed to forget how the eldest son's freedom had been obtained. He was free—his body could not be whipped, he was not in danger of being murdered like Juan the Gardener or Alicax, Miguel's arms and legs were not shackled in irons like the companions left behind—but the price, the price of that liberation, was a life mortgaged for years to come.

That was the explanation he gave himself and others for breaking that promise to deliver the letters, an explanation that, throughout these eighteen years as he dragged that burden in his bag like a lame leg in the dust, and limped from one misfortune to the next one, I had no reason to doubt.

Until that first night in the Sevilla jail, when his past was laid out, bare as a corpse, for me to examine, and I came to realize that the story was more complicated.

The real motive: he had found it impossible to distribute the letters because he could not face the relatives, had no answer to the question that their eyes, perhaps even their lips, would inevitably formulate: *why you, why not him, why not my Beltrán, our Pablo?* He would have to lie to them about the chances of survival of Diego and José, of Gonzalo and Santiago, pledge to rescue them, promising to raise the funds to lead an expedition bound to fail, giving the wife false hope and the children the illusion that they would see their father alive once more. Or would it be more compassionate to simply tell them, *your man is never coming home, it's time to start a new life without being chained forever to the irreparable past*?

It was what I had been suggesting to him from the very start, that he stop incessantly evoking the sting of the captivity he had suffered and that those other friends were still suffering. That must have been the reason, I suppose, why I had appeared inside him, precisely coinciding with the moment of his liberation, so I could beckon with my song and thirst for adventure, *you've been away for ten years and need to make up for all you didn't eat, all the people you never met, all the books you didn't read, all the books you did not get to write, the greatness that attends you*.

And yet, despite my incitement to turn the page on the past, he had not forgotten his own pain nor the existence of those men. The proof was in those sobs that overcame him as he finished Alonzo's letter to Amparo.

Sobs also of relief. Because suddenly, accidentally, unexpectedly, miraculously, Sevilla was giving him the chance to compensate for those abandoned captives, offset what he owed to them. Here were letters again, except these would most certainly be delivered, would serve their purpose. Alonzo was only the first of many doomed men, Amparo the first of many widows, Cervantes came to the realization that he was fated to be a secretary for the dead.

Not only for the dead, as he was to discover very soon indeed. Papa Pasamonte passed by a bit before dawn to see how the writing was going, sat himself down in a corner of the cell and demanded to hear the letters he had been instrumental in having assigned to the newcomer. Papa Pasamonte wanted to check the merchandise.

The first letter, to Teresa Clavijo, asking for mercy, met with his resounding approval. The second one made him frown.

"You know, Miguel, when you die, it's called the day of reckoning. The day you finally pay the bill. But when you pay that bill, you're a fool if you don't remember how much you enjoyed the meal and that special way the wine growled in your throat—and you can repent of having screwed too many women but you can't take back the pleasure it gave you. Or them. Or them! This—this last message to Amparo, it's a beauty, Miguel, there's no denying you're a born poet. But you know what? Overly sad. The people in this building, me included, me especially, we have plenty to be sorry for, sorry for what we did and sorry for what we will never get to do because of bad luck or stupid mistakes or just ignorance. But anyone—any priest, any third-rate scribbler with a sentimental tune—can make you cry, but only a genius can take the ruins of a life and make you smile. So tell you what. I want you to make Amparo laugh. That's what you're being paid for. There are enough terrible times ahead, solitary nights crying into her pillow, I wouldn't be surprised if she and her three daughters end up homeless, out on the streets, plenty to make her bread bitter without you adding an extra layer of wretchedness. I want her to remember the good times she had with Alonzo, the jokes they exchanged, I want her to think of him dying defiantly, with his head held high, undefeated, as if he were still beating the drum as he marched his mates into the caverns of death. Use that phrase, my phrase, the caverns of death. Better still, don't even mention death, the Hell with my phrase. So you spruce this goddamn thing up, Miguel—because you have it in you, don't tell me you're not able to find the joy. If you can't find some joy to transmit to her, or to anybody else who, if I give the go ahead, will soon be clamoring for your services, if you're just mourning and moping and full of guilt shit, I tell you, then you're not the man we need. But I can read character. Like you can read books, well, I can read you, I know you're not just this sorrow that has come streaming out from who knows from where, though I suspect from where, won't even try to tell you what you already know. So, here's what we're going to do. I trust you enough that I won't need to come by to certify how you've altered this letter before you read it to Alonzo a few hours from now. Keep some grief, that's all right, you shouldn't treat this with levity, the man is going to have his tongue sticking out of his mouth and his face will turn blue and he'll have piss and shit running down his legs, so we're not going to lie about this tragedy and all, but you will give this letter wings so Amparo can fly, can return to it the rest of her life and fly with the wings of words you've given her."

I could have applauded Papa Pasamonte, kissed him on both cheeks and even on the mouth, I could not have expressed it better, had been looking for almost two decades for someone to lighten Miguel up, prepare him for my existence and the great task ahead.

And Cervantes, no fool, realized that if he did not comply he might not survive the savagery of the Sevilla jail, but, perhaps more crucially, was in danger of succumbing to self-pity and gloom, killing that best part of himself without which he could not write anything worthwhile, not ever.

He did as he was told, spruced up the letter to Amparo, lightened it up, made Alonzo smile, allowed him to die one week later with those jubilant words in his heart as he mounted the scaffold.

And when Pasamonte recounted to Cervantes how that letter had consoled the widow, he resolved, then and there, that if ever he was released from this Cárcel de Sevilla, he would take upon himself the task of finding the relatives of the doomed captives of Algiers. Dispersed though they might be all over Spain, he would find them and enchant them with the remote syllables of their loved ones.

Did it matter if that farfetched resolution was unsustainable, that he was doubtlessly deceiving himself? If it let him start banishing the ghosts that haunted his spirit, if it fortified our author to face the next needy inmate with elation rather than grief, who was I to puncture that particular reverie?

In effect, the letters that followed that decision became easier. He was inspired by the prisoners themselves. Yes, they were remorseful, yes, they spent hours with Padre de León and other priests confessing every last felony and disciplining themselves with rods and mortifying themselves to contain the demons of excessive self-love, yes, they wished to meet their Lord purged of any depravity, yes, they prayed until their knees bled—but when they spoke to Cervantes, they uncovered another, more luminous zone and, as per Papa Pasamonte's instructions, he guided them there. And they responded to that help by helping him. I noted how, story by story, day by day, letter by letter, the burden of those undelivered letters he was carrying seemed to lessen the more he became the secretary of life and for life and with life.

I was all for it. I could see how he was feeding off the stories he was being told, unaware that he was making his way towards me, slowly growing into the man I needed to be in order to be given birth from the ashes of the old Cervantes. Rather than a victim beset with the sickness of silence, here was my Miguel stretching and warming up the muscles of his creativity, watering his adjectives, making his verbs blossom, becoming bolder, more motivated, honing a style that had gathered rust during those long forlorn periods of mute wandering. Indispensable, these new exercises of prose if he were ever to write the masterpiece that both he and I and Zahara herself had so glowingly predicted.

And he was on his way, he was, he was. As his fame increased—or should I modestly call it his reputation, given that I envisage real renown, real prominence in the future only once he lets me victoriously preside over his life—people from outside the prison began to inquire about his expertise. A young nobleman who had been cheated out of his inheritance by his deceased father's second wife craved someone to convince the judges to rule in his favor—and Miguel's eloquence did the trick, and furthermore elicited tears from the eyes of spectators and even the wicked defendant's lawyer. And then a couple of former *cautivos* wondered if Master Cervantes would be willing to write a petition begging the King and the Privy Council to reward their many years of dedication to the kingdom and the cause of the Catholic Church. After interviewing both petitioners at length, he agreed to accept the *encargo*, aware that their chances were even slimmer than his had been when he had sent several *requisitorias* upon his return from Algiers without ever receiving anything other than perfunctory answers and, naturally, no restitution. Several stories they told him did not seem to correspond entirely to his own experiences, these petitioners appeared to exaggerate exploits and overemphasize miseries, but he gave them the benefit of the doubt. They had suffered like he had, like the men whose letters he kept at the bottom of his bag, and he did for these new comrades what nobody had thought to do for him upon his return, my Miguel had a far too generous heart.

A generous heart and a purse that cried out for endless replenishing: they paid well, these and others who came to consult him from outside the black walls of the jail.

Not that Miguel was greedy. He was always careful to give Papa Pasamonte his cut, always careful to keep him content. Going so far as to make his protector into an accomplice of his renewed skills and intellectual aspirations, by casting the baldheaded giant in the main roles of two small interludes, *entremeses*, somewhat scandalous playlets, that he wrote and staged in the central hall of the prison for the entertainment— and edification, he hastened to assure Padre de León and the Head Warden—of the inmates.

But my author's true literary ambitions were only fully expressed in what he scribbled down for nobody but himself. During these months, the prisoners, those who are to die and those who will at some point be released, the Basques and the Catalans, the Cordobeses and the men of La Mancha, all of Spain intersecting in this jail, have emptied out their hearts and their exploits to him in painstaking, at times rowdy sessions of remembrance. He is less interested in those who have been falsely accused and are innocent, than in the others,

murderers and thieves and falsifiers, heretics and blasphem-
ers and necromancers, prostitutes and panderers and cheats,
and over and over the sodomites and their *pecado nefando*,
their abominable and unspeakable sin.

He gobbles up all those sinuous memories, transforms
them into coherence, seeking beauty and elegance and clo-
sure where there is only a mess of tangled threads and blind
alleys, he looks for the pulse of their motives, how their minds
work to justify the worse deeds. What they were thinking at
the moment of their crime, not now, not in retrospect, not as
death and eternal punishment loom ahead, but also retroac-
tively. "Why did you thrust your sword so swiftly into that
prostitute's throat, why the silver chalice in the Church and
not the one made of gold, what held you back from the more
valuable object, when the wrong man came along on the road
to Carmona, that poor silk vendor, why did you rob and kill
him anyway, were you aware that the boy you enticed with
sweets under the fig trees was only twelve. How did you trick
that Genovese banker out of his goods?"

Padre de León wants to reform those lost souls, is obsessed
with making them better, will use all his powers of persua-
sion and fear to wash their sins away, praise them for showing
contrition and lashing themselves, the good Padre trying to
convince these reprobates that the best thing that could have
happened to them was to get caught so they would lapse no
more and gain eternal salvation. But for Cervantes, the regrets
extracted in this way seem to him less sincere than the wild
desires of those men and women. He loves them as they are,
lies and all, he understands that we are created as much by the
fabrications we invent for ourselves as by the hard truth we

will finally awaken to, loves the distance between what these clients dreamt for their future selves and the painful, incarcerated reality of where they have ended up.

He has a prodigious ability to step outside the boundaries of his self, and step into the shoes of those sinners, an immense compassion for all of them. But the ones that most attract him, almost unhealthily, are the ones who do not repent, who defy the pressure to cry and wail on the way to the gibbet, he admires the serenity with which they refuse to lament the lives of sin and liberty they have led. The inspiration he truly thirsts for nestles in the recalcitrant, the rebellious, the ones who, unafraid of ridicule, don't care what anyone thinks of them, the stubborn souls who rise up from the ground every time they are beaten down.

If he starts to judge them, he will never get to touch the bittersweet truth of who they are. His voraciousness knows no limits. He seeks—and is told—much more than fits into the farewell letters. At times his clients complain that so much material, anecdotes, and tricks, have not been included in those messages they are paying for, and Cervantes explains the omissions away effortlessly: space is lacking or maybe, he tells them, some parts of their less worthy confessions are not suited for the families or the world to know, might damage the honorable image they want to leave behind.

What he does not tell them is that many of those tales discarded from the letters sent to loved ones are accumulated with avid stealth on scraps of paper, transcripts that he rewrites assiduously, giving them a more graceful and long-lasting literary form. Nor does he mention that he questions Padre de León about the lives of former prisoners, who had long since been strung up and hung, tied to the stake and burned to cinders, whipped and decapitated.

Perhaps he fears that the clients could well ask him, why such a passion for trawling, why stuff page after page with those ragtag sketches and memories, why, what for, with what purpose?

I asked myself the same questions. It's true I was gladdened by his enthusiasm—anything to slacken his despondency, especially if it entailed writing—but at the same time I was concerned by this maniacal fixation with the misery of others, worried that he could be sucked into the vortex of a perversity he seemed to relish too much. Until one evening some weeks ago just before Christmas, I came to understand what was going on.

It was during a dinner hosted by Padre Pedro de León, an event that has become habitual when the good Jesuit is in residence, rather than on some mission to close brothels in Málaga, or convert thirty-six English pirates from Protestantism. I tend to enjoy those encounters between Cervantes and his friend in a room on the third floor of the prison, next to the chapel, I like their philosophical banter and camaraderie, but above all I always hope that, by eavesdropping on Pedro and Miguel, I'll be able to extract some tidbit of information or clue that can help me make sense of what is materializing in the mind that Cervantes often keeps shuttered.

Usually I don't learn much I don't already know, but on that one occasion, I was offered a surprise. Which started to manifest itself midway through that frugal meal of lentils and bacon when Padre Pedro de León suddenly said to Cervantes: "You know what's wrong with you, Miguel? You care more about the stories of these poor men and women than about their salvation."

I have discovered that it does not take much to make my dear author pass from serenity to anger, and could sense, even before he responded, that he did not take this criticism well. In effect, he launched into one of his diatribes: "Just because I don't mount the scaffold with them, press the crucifix into their hands, wipe their tears away, ask them to pardon the executioner who is merely following orders, merely doing his job, just because I don't whisper to them to quell any raging or covetous thought before the rope snaps their neck or the fire is kindled, the knife finds the unwilling throat, Pedro, doesn't mean I don't care. Oh, I have seen enough death, enough blood to last me five thousand lifetimes, I have seen enough cruelty and piercings, it is not my job to ask anybody to purify their body by making it suffer more with self-flagellation and bruised knees. I love the body I was given, crippled as it is, I love this world, I love these prisoners. Or are you envious that I know more about them than you do—all you care about are their faults, whereas me—tell me, tell me what sort of stew Enriqueta García cooked for her parents before she left them for a life of wantonness, tell me the secret of the recipe, tell me what Gaspar Solapo's youngest son (do you even know his name?) exclaimed when he saw his father fly that first kite near that field in La Mancha, tell me the story of the two wives of Vicente Toledano, both of whom needed letters sent to them. The truth, they tell me the truth, the full extent of their *fechorías* and the coils of their lasciviousness, what they hide from you, *querido Padre*, pretending they are innocent because they hope you'll put in a good word for them and negotiate their release or a mitigation of the penalty. Even when they are walked down the last street on the donkey, even as they hear the *pregonero* announcing to all of Sevilla the reasons why they have been condemned, they still hold out hope that you will intervene, not to save their souls, but their bodies, their imperfect, pulsating bodies. And when the trapdoor opens or they smell the flame burning close by, it is my words that will provide comfort. And you say I don't care about them?"

Padre de León did not lose his usual unruffled demeanor, not for an instant.

"The very vehemence of your reaction suggests that I have hit a sensitive spot. Because you have not answered me. For what purpose, Miguel, why, what do you intend to do with those lives that have been entrusted to you? It is not so you can rescue their souls from the captivity of sin. This you have admitted, that you are more fascinated with what their imperfect, pulsating bodies desire. I will not apologize for doing what I can for the eternal rest of those souls. Maybe you should follow my example and not apologize, not even feel you have to defend what you are doing for . . . . What? What are you planning, Miguel—you were always planning something as a young lad, what mischief are you dreaming of now?"

And Cervantes calmed down as instantly as he had heated up, Cervantes essayed something between a grin and a grimace and admitted that he was . . . He intended to write a picaresque novel.

No, I thought to myself, this is not right, I thought, as he proceeded to explain, bashfully at first and then with swelling confidence, why this was the ideal channel for his talents and manias, no, no, I said to him, quietly at first and then with swelling apprehension, this is not what you were born to do, what Zahara expects of you, why I have stayed loyally by your side for almost two decades, I said it to him as he described how a wandering *pícaro* protagonist would allow him to visit all the corners of a Spain that had lost its way and moral compass, and is drowning in a bottomless ocean of corruption. The humorous anecdotes and misfortunes that befall that person driven to crime by poverty, once every legitimate door of advancement and recognition has been slammed in his face, would illuminate the reader, no, no, no, I almost shouted, this is not the novel you are meant to write, that I have watched you prepare for, that your style has been anticipating here in this jail, no, no, no, Miguel, don't make that mistake, while he insisted on how he wanted a book full of life and vitality and bursting with the real men and women of his land, of the ordinary sort you find in the *ventas* and on the road and at court and in the villages, pilgrims and cattle herders, *bachilleres* and barbers, silk merchants and scullery maids, a picaresque novel would be the perfect mirror into which our fellow countrymen could peer and see themselves and laugh at their image and also question who they are and where in Hell they were going.

"A critique?" Padre Pedro de León asked. "Like the two *entremeses* you put on recently and that I had to—"

"I'll be more careful, Pedro," Miguel had answered. "That was just for fun, just to amuse the prisoners, to let Pasamonte prove that he is a great performer."

"If I hadn't intervened afterwards, one of my colleagues in the priesthood, a Dominican, I need not repeat his name, he would have reported you to the authorities, who knows how I could have shielded you from the Holy Brotherhood of the Inquisition if they came calling. And if you were to write something similar in this new novel, something so unbridled, that so transgresses every norm, then nobody will be able to protect you. I believe you when you say you'll be careful, I'm sure you'll find a way to be ironical and not direct, mask some of your sharpest opinions, couch it all in acceptable terms. But that's the least of your worries. I have here . . . ." And Padre de León rose from his seat at the table and walked over to a bookcase, coming back with a thick set of pages, "I have here a novel by Mateo Alemán. Guess what's in it? Guess what Mateo, who spent all those months in here, just like you, doing your same letter-writing job, guess what Mateo, once he was free, guess into what he decided to fritter away his energy? A picaresque novel, Miguel, that's what. His protagonist, Guzmán de Alfarache, does everything you say you want yours to accomplish—and his work is superb, my friend, saturated with wit and bitter observations and a whole array of criminals, the criminals who commit every vice imaginable and the criminals governing us who create the conditions for those poor souls to indulge in such iniquities. He's beat you to it. It will be published next year—to acclaim and popularity, I assure you, the best book of that sort since the *Lazarillo*, and more ethical, because Guzmán at the end sees the light, repents, understands that all his misadventures and swindles have been part of the dream of life, he ends up disenchanted and chastised, he awakens to the only truth of our stay here on earth, the preparation for the eternal goodness of God. And that's why it's been approved for publication by our ailing King and, just as significantly, by the Inquisition, by the Archbishop, by everybody who is anybody, given permission to circulate and thrive. So, if I were you, dear Miguel, I would steer clear of the picaresque. By all means, dabble in it here and there, use some of the stories you have drawn out of these men on their way to death—that is between you and your conscience—you can incorporate them into some other literary work that your *ingenio* may come up with, but a whole novel? Stay out of trouble, look for something else to make yourself famous."

I was ecstatic at this reaction from such a prestigious ally, though knowing Miguel . . .

"My novel will be better," he said sullenly. "I have stories that Mateo would kill for, ideas he would cut his hand off to have conceived, a gentle style and flow and prick of the pen that he will envy. I will not back down, I will not."

So it's natural that he has not backed down since then, has continued collecting stories undeterred, has kept listening attentively to his clients and taking copious notes. I wasn't surprised by how he persisted on this disastrous course, because my hopes that Padre de León's sermon would have some effect had been swiftly undermined by a comment Cervantes had let fall at the end of that revelatory dinner, "It doesn't have to be a man, you know, Pedro."

"What, who doesn't have to be a man, what are you talking about?"

"The hero of my novel could be a heroine, doesn't have to be a man, could be a woman, right, that would be different, that would leave Mateo panting by the wayside, don't you think?"

Pedro de León thought that was an even worse idea.

The good Jesuit would be even more offended if he were with us now, a few weeks after the dinner, this morning of

January 5th, if he could hear the conversation that Miguel de Cervantes is having with Constanza Salvadora, la Pícara Constanza, she of the long razor blade in her pocket and whose adventures Cervantes has been listening to during long and juicy sessions. Now he leans close to her, asking her to speak in low murmurs so Marín and Garrido and Carrasco cannot hear a word, though they show no inclination to do so, waiting their turn from a respectful distance.

Constanza has a serious problem, in fact, more than one. And, thanks to Cervantes, more than one possible solution.

Around a month ago, a *soplón* had let the Alcaide know—hoping to get his two hundred lashes significantly reduced—that a large contingent of women had been snuck into the jail to spend a night of abandonment and pleasure with assorted inmates, ninety-nine to be more exact. "Ninety-nine?" the Alcaide had demanded of the stool-pigeon and the man had nodded his head with more enthusiasm than was being expended by the female bodies harbored in the largest cell upstairs. But when the Alcaide had invaded that huge dormitory on the second floor, he and his acolytes found nothing—all the prisoners in their respective cots covered with their respective and respectful blankets. Because, of course, when the lookouts reported that the guards were marching up the steps, the ladies had hidden under those blankets, were even glad to cuddle there, close to the object of their desire.

The Alcaide had left the scene, embarrassed and enraged, and had been about to double the *soplón*'s punishment to four hundred lashes, when the man begged him to look under the covers, his information was accurate, the visit had been arranged by the notorious Constanza Salvadora.

"Constanza Salvadora?" The warden was scornful. "There is a warrant out for her arrest for a year now, how could she possibly be in this Cárcel?"

"What better place to hide," the stoolie smirked, "than the jail where you all have been trying to convey her, who would think to search here? Go upstairs again, lay bare the men and expose the women and among them will be the famous *ladrona,* Constanza Salvadora—you'll be successful, I guarantee it, or you can triple my punishment to six hundred strokes."

And, in effect, the blankets were stripped, the ladies were dragged from their lovers, those who were whores were severely chastised, those who were married to men of eminence were scurried away to avoid further disrepute, those who were supposedly virgins ended up being mended by Celestinas in order not to spoil their upcoming wedding nights, and Constanza Salvadora, Constanza had been taken into custody and sentenced to die by hanging because of her many thefts and refractory concupiscence, not to mention her latest mammoth whore-mongering venture. And indeed, is to die unless . . . unless Cervantes finds a way out.

He has written two letters on her behalf last night and now reads them to her. The first is directed to Doña Brígida Corzo, the esteemed, rich and virtuous wife of Juan Antonio Corzo. The main benefactress of the poorest inmates in the Cárcel, she pleads for them and feeds their ravenous bellies, sending them bread and vegetables as well as a colossal copper container where half a cow fits. More significantly, she has promised forty ducats to any woman ready to break free from the public houses and piously marry some good Christian. Thanks to the many stories Constanza has been recounting to him for days, Miguel has found, concealed in her past, a man willing to make an honest woman of this repentant sinner—as long as the future husband is rewarded with a substantial dowry. And such a ceremony, where both Doña Brígida and her Juan Antonio would officiate as godmother and godfather, would do much to soften the hearts of the judges who, helped by a handsome bribe, would surely spare this converted damsel's life and the new spouse from affliction and, more relevantly, flatter such powerful and prosperous sponsors.

The second letter is meant to make this mitigation of the sentence amenable by paying back the considerable sums that Constanza has stolen and that led to the original warrant for her arrest. For this, Cervantes has turned to Cristóbal Garay, a Sevilla loan shark that he has recurred to whenever he found himself unable to reimburse gambling debts. To Cristóbal, rather than exalting the Christian qualities of a remorseful Constanza, Cervantes paints an opulent, luxuriant, lush picture of this future wife and how many *reales*, once free, she could breathlessly bring in by day and by night, her many contacts and astute wheelings and dealings. An excellent investment of capital, more so if Garay were also guaranteed access to her assets and attributes.

Constanza is profusely thankful. Cervantes refuses any payment. He has already milked her of many stories and does not need her to milk him for pleasure in the ways she is accustomed to—all that he asks is that, if they let her go, she continue to visit him from time to time to recount her past life and any interesting anecdotes from what he presumes will be a fruitful marriage and its related activities. As an advance bonus, she now offers him the tale of how she arranged for the mulatto Isidro Solís to marry seven different *putas* on separate occasions, so he could receive (with a fat percentage for Constanza) the dowries assigned to each of them by a benevolent abbot. Isidro was caught and garroted for this flagrant abuse of the sacrament of marriage, but without ever revealing who had been his intermediary and procurer, bless his heart.

"Just make sure," she says to Miguel, eyeing Marín, Garrido and Carrasco, "that when you write about this, as seems to be your intention, my name is not divulged—unless, of course, I am dead, in which case I wish that my deeds and achievements be trumpeted to all four winds."

"You can trust me," he answers.

They part the best of friends. And now, yes, at last, he motions to the three men who step forward with docile gestures and bows that cannot disguise, as far as I am concerned, their hypocrisy.

"So, gentlemen," Miguel de Cervantes smiles at each of them, "what can I do for you?"

How can he not see that they are bent on revenge, how can he be so blind? How can he not realize these villains have come here to destroy him?

FIVE

" ... Don Fernando asked the captive to tell them the story of
his life, which was bound to be interesting . . . . To which the
captive responded that he would gladly do as he was asked:
*And that way, your graces will hear a true account that will
surpass the lying fictions which tend to be composed with such
strange and planned artifice.*"

—*Don Quixote de la Mancha*

"WE HAVE A problem," Marín says.

"And if you," Garrido adds, "help us solve it . . ."

"We will reciprocate."

"Lately," the *escribano* Carrasco intervenes, "Spain's coun-
cils and magistrates and adjudicators and, alas, notaries, have
been inundated with a plethora, I use the word appropriately,
I trust, in the presence of a scholar such as yourself, Miguel
de Cervantes, whether Cortinas or Saavedra, as you now call
yourself, always so erudite and perceptive, a plethora, I repeat,
of petitions and stories and requests and narratives and tales
from all kinds of former captives."

"Or rather," Marín corrected him, "people who claim to
be former captives. And the workload, to be blunt, is getting
to be cumbersome—endlessly corroborating evidence, does
this date match that one, has this suffering been exaggerated
or even invented, oh it's so tedious."

"And frankly, driving us a bit crazy. All this gathering of
witnesses, the same questions over and over. Unexciting,
dull, humdrum. Stopping us from the more important work

required for the security and surveillance of our realm and dominions—like finding people such as you for missions like that one to the coast of Berbería, I'm sure you're still grateful for that opportunity, like this one, to serve Spain."

Spain! Again and again, Spain! Yet again the offer, the urge, the command, to serve the country from which he had felt estranged upon his return. And to which he had remained loyal, in spite of his frustration. Something he had discussed with Padre Pedro de León one evening when his schooldays friend remarked on how much Miguel had changed from the boy he recalled, funny and exuberant and eager for what life would beget.

"Changed?" Miguel paused, as if wondering whether to let the moment pass or if . . . . Then, seemingly out of nowhere, he let loose a torrent of recriminations: "Not me, not me. The country, they changed my country while I was away. At first, Pedro, at first I told myself that I was to blame, the one who was out of step. It hurt too much not to fit into the country, how it dreamt itself. So I simply made believe that everything was the same, that ten years made no difference in the life of a nation, it had to be my fault, captivity had displaced me, that's what I told myself. And for years closed my eyes, kept repeating that we were the greatest empire in the world, that we still are. Refused to accept that we were going down the drain. Owners of half the orb and going down the drain. Wars abroad and beggars at home and the few rich and the far too many poor and we expel those who are different and we silence those who are critical, down, down, down the drain, how could I possibly accept that this was permanently true? Everything I touched was, at first glance, unaltered—the smell of bread in the morning, the way the birds wing their song, the laughter from a tavern, the evening fog of Madrid, everything seemed the same, the walls of my fatherland. But inside, those walls had crumbled, it was mere smoke and mirage and appearance, inside the walls were hollow. And nobody seemed to notice. As if they were all enchanted. As if under a . . . a spell. As if a sorcerer had flown in and left the façade of every object and locale and color outwardly intact, but swept away what really mattered, the soul and sound of things, left us all stumbling among phantoms. You know what Spain is, Pedro? A land of people who can't stand the truth about themselves and thus a land from which we can't escape. Easier to escape from Algiers and its dungeons than from a world where we are apparently free, but not free of our blindness and desire. How to escape from blindness when you tell yourself you can see, how can you escape from desire when you're incessantly told the lie that the world and its riches and pleasures are there for the taking? Lies, all lies. And you know what is saddest, Pedro? If they come to me again asking me to serve Spain, disenchanted as I may be, I will say yes, that is what is saddest of all. Because, like everybody in this jail and in this captive jail of a country, like you and each man and woman breathing our air, I am ready to be fooled again and again. I will do my duty, if they come to ask me, I will dance to their tune once more."

And now, here were these men, putting his words to the test, tempting him. As if they knew his weak spot.

"Not only does Spain need you," says Marín. "Also His Majesty, so unfortunately ill of late."

"But still vigilant."

"Still vigilant, and envisaging, as always, assistance from his loyal subjects. So we thought we'd set up an office dedicated to reducing these infinite supplications to a trickle, separate the true from the false, the wheat from the chaff with ... well, a winnowing fork like the one John the Baptist used, an office where we could install you."

"Why you?" the notary Carrasco asked rhetorically. "It was my idea. Because you were instrumental in writing requests for aid on behalf of two *cautivos*—and their versions turned out to be, after considerable checking and rechecking and counter-checking, they turned out to be, overall, with an embellishment here and an enhancement there, to be verifiable, you had shown ethical standards, only working for those who had indeed been held hostage and warranted at least some sort of commendation. And so I said, why not return to this Cervantes whom we have already vetted, who can save us time and treasure and pick over the candidates, weed out the dishonorable ones?"

"Why not, indeed?" echoed Marín. "An expert in captivity, specializing in suffering and survival, he can do the job, rid us of the bad seeds, save us a ton of trouble—and, hey, save my marriage. I get home so tired at night from listening to these stories, all of them the same, boring myself to death and then unable to even read the latest book of chivalry to the wife, who's eager to find out what's up with the grown son of Belianís. And that's why ..."

"And that's why," Garrido said, "we're here today in this palace of justice and equanimity. Upstairs, in the room next to the infirmary, the one where you habitually have dinner with

Reverend Padre de León—oh yes, we know that and lots more about your activities—in that very room, given that the saintly father is away on who knows what holy business, Esteban Estudillo awaits you."

"He's come to us with quite a story, rather on the implausible side, to put it mildly."

"A swindler, that's what we suspect he is."

"But what if he's telling the truth? We haven't been captives, thank God: all our knowledge is secondhand, through people like you. And you are proof that, after all, we live in an epoch when the most extraordinary things happen to the most ordinary of people, where we cannot rule out marvelous and inexplicable events coming to pass."

"Who better than you to decide his fate?"

For the first time, Cervantes spoke: "I am to judge him then?"

I can tell he's hooked, he's interested, he's falling into their laps, their trap, don't do it, tell them to go to Hell, Miguel, tell them you will not collaborate in any of their schemes!

Marín smiles. "Wouldn't that be refreshing? Getting to dole out a sentence, guilty or innocent, instead of always being on the receiving end? Don't say you aren't attracted by such an opportunity?"

"So long as you can be neutral, objective, fair, balanced," Carrasco interjects, with a pleading look on his face. "Because you're going to like old Esteban, this Estudillo, he's like his surname, a student of everything, he loves to read, can't get him to stop, an educated fellow, like you, Cervantes, so be careful not to let that sway you in his favor."

"And I will be alone with him?"

"If that's what you need to draw him out, you seem to be pretty good at that, according to our sources. You listen to Esteban's tale, then deliver your verdict, if he should be given a good beating and put in jail for fraudulently trying to cheat His Majesty's servants, by pretending to have endured slavery and torments that never existed ..."

"Or if, on the contrary, he should be afforded some hard-earned assistance."

"And once my mission has been completed?"

"If we are satisfied that you have indeed, effectively and sincerely, accomplished what you rightly call your mission, then you will walk out of this jail today and this very afternoon we'll set you up in a room full of ample windows where, tomorrow morning, you can start meeting up with *cautivos*, whether simulating or trustworthy, *falsos o verdaderos*, you'll decide, this one bound for glory, this one a kick in the ass. For which service, you will receive a small fee, food and lodgings paid for, and some hours off each day to pursue your literary fervors."

"Literary fervors which, we presume, will not deviate from the doctrine of our Holy Mother the Church."

"The initial contract is to last for a year ...."

"Because, that's how long," Carrasco explained, always seeming to side with Cervantes, "it will take for the charges against you to be dropped, that's what Judge Gaspar de Vallejo has vowed if you decide to contribute to this patriotic cause."

"That contract can be renewed yearly, of course, with a significant increase in your stipend and free time. Our way of making sure that we don't deprive our Golden Age of an author whose promise we predicted from the start and has made such a name for himself in this jail that you are soon to quit."

"What say you, good sir? Do we have a deal?"

Cervantes does not answer immediately, lets a long minute tick by. He seems to be waiting for something, for somebody, for anybody to whisper advice in his ear, a comrade who can weigh the pros and cons of this offer objectively. For me? Can he be waiting for me to help him?

Very well, Miguel, if that's what you require at this critical juncture, I will gallop heroically to the rescue, I shall not fail you. Here's what I think, here's what is best for you, here's what—that he should, of course, embrace this opportunity to seek refuge in a room lit up by the sun, where, far from this suffocating confinement and the demands of Papa Pasamonte and endless reading sessions of books by other authors, he can write and write and write to his heart's content.

That is what I should tell him, but for some reason I cannot, not a word of encouragement comes out of my mind and mouth, I who have always coveted an occasion when I could intervene in the contours of his destiny.

It is not merely that all this sounds suspicious, the terms far too favorable, the pledges of these ruffians not to be trusted. No, something else paralyzes and confuses me, stops my tongue.

Something else, something else: I cannot ignore that if he accepts that offer of liberty, he won't be using it to give me life but to start the picaresque novel in which I do not fit, that damn picaresque novel which endangers my prospects. I cannot ignore that if he barely listens to me now, he will be even less inclined to do so once, freed from jail, he can center all his attention on the adventures of some scoundrel or prostitute.

He will write to his heart's content, but not to mine. Mine is, right now, full of dread and sorrow. Not dread or sorrow for him, as has been my wont since I first kept him company. Dread for me, sorrow for my fate, the neglect and slow withering I see lurking in the months and years ahead until I disappear completely from his horizon.

Is he so much in love with his picaresque characters? Let them counsel him, let them approach him with their wisdom, if they have any. Not me. Not me?

Can I be thinking this, admitting this? Someone like me, who has always prized himself as being noble and faithful, a good friend, always ready to be happy for my Miguel, can I be conceiving, let alone expressing, such disloyal words? Is this the naked truth about me, what has been lurking inside my most intimate fears and longing, what is now unmasked?

That I am not that good friend, cannot be happy for him. That faced with the possibility of my own extinction, what I yearn for is that Miguel de Cervantes remain in this miserable prison until he has kept faith with me, until he has given me the birth I deserve.

There it is, then, this is who I am, what I have been brought to, perhaps who I always was and have been. I do not like to separate his heart from mine, I do not like the despondency and craving that are adulterating me—as I did not like the jealousy I felt when Zahara embraced my Miguel—but I cannot deny what this emergency has revealed and made of me, somebody so desperate to be born that he cares only for himself and falls shamefully silent when he should speak out.

And so it is that, tainted with self-interest, shocked at my own lack of generosity, I say nothing, I refuse to give advice to

Cervantes when he is most at risk, I withdraw into myself, so it is, so it is that, lapsing into a sullen sort of stillness, I let my author decide on his own, and exercise that freedom he keeps vaunting as the most precious of human possessions, so it is that, conflicted and torn, part of me wanting him to succeed in something he so desires and part of me wanting him to fail in something that may lead to disaster for both of us, and all of me wary of the intentions of these three dreadful seducers, so it is that I passively watch Cervantes consent to that poison-ous proposal, of course he does, and I can do nothing other than to mutely follow him and that satanic trio up two flights of stairs into the room where we find that man, Esteban Estu-dillo, reading one of Padre de León's books, his thin back to us, entranced by whatever universe he is plunged into.

The interlopers call out his name. When he turns towards us, I get my first glimpse of him, tall and emaciated and some-how strangely familiar, with the sickly, jaundiced look of a man who has spent too many hours and *jornadas* away from the sun, it's as if I had seen him somewhere, met him at some point, but where, how? Marín snaps his fingers and the man springs up like a dog who's been whipped much too often, and closes the book and, clasping it to his breast as if afraid it will be snatched away by demons, starts pacing back and forth, playing with his shadow, back and forth, back and forth, until he sits himself down in a corner, head twitching and legs quivering.

No sooner have Marín, Garrido and Carrasco left him alone with us, than Esteban immediately changes his attitude, sidling up to Cervantes and moaning, "They don't believe me, they have never dipped their little toe in the Mediterranean or withstood the darkness of the dungeons of Istanbul, and they dare to mock me, make sinister insinuations, help me, help me, good sir. Help me or they will beat me again, they will hurt me."

Miguel de Cervantes puts him at ease with a joke and a story of how he had himself been assailed by these three men, how their bark was worse than their bite, and all Señor Estudillo needed to do was tell the truth and all would be well, Cervantes would defend him as if he were an orphan.

"Is that a promise, sir?" the old man asks, his eyes watery and weary. "Can you swear it on the woman you love and serve, sir, the one you have always been faithful to, at least in your heart?"

"You have my word," Cervantes responds firmly. "I will let no further harm come to you."

Esteban must have sensed that he could trust this man who was going to decide his destiny, he must have read the kindness in Miguel's eyes, because it did not take long for a tale of woe and calamity to gush from his mouth, a tale that was, indeed, as incredible as the three men had proclaimed.

Esteban began with his noble birth and his thirst for travel, leading to a shipwreck during which he rescued a young, virginal woman from the waves, and swum her to a providentially nearby beach where they were attracted to each other despite her protestations that she was no more than a lowly swineherd—and he had only found out later through a letter that she carried that she was an Albanian princess fleeing from a marriage that her evil stepmother had arranged to get her away from the father who adored her. And their vows of eternal fidelity would be measured and taxed when French pirates captured and sold them, Esteban to the Turks and his darling Clarisea to merchants who were heading, it seemed, for some icy dukedom in the far north of the earth. But this terrible trick of fortune would not stop him from finding her. After a fight that would put Theagenes to shame—he could show his wounds, his broken teeth, the cuts on his back—his captors had cast him in irons and transported him to Istanbul, where he had shown such wisdom that the Great Sultan's Vizier had elevated him to the rank of councilor and offered him a brilliant career if only he converted to Islam. But he had refused this temptation—*helped by the voice of Santo Domingo each night imploring me not to relent*—and an even loftier temptation when the wife of this high official had fallen in love with him, but he, Esteban Estudillo, would not renounce his faith nor would he betray Clarisea, using instead the infatuation of the Vizier's wife to escape. He had fooled her into thinking he would take her with him and had left her high and dry, but he had not been dry or high, but wet and low, because on his way to Spain, perhaps because God wanted to punish him for lying to a lady, no matter if she were an infidel, his ship had been boarded by Berbers. He had escaped another captivity by jumping into the sea—"the sea, the sea always haunts me, its eternal murmur"—managing to swim ashore in Sicily, where for once Lady Luck proved to be on his side this time. He landed near a town that his own long lost cousin had conquered from the Turk, and he had helped this relative to foil a plot engineered by evil courtiers and as a reward had been dispatched on a ship that, though buffeted by further storms, transported him safely to a port in Catalonia. And now, now, all he needed was for the King to grant him some assistance so he could find his beloved princess. He would track her down to the ends of the earth, even if it turned out she was not of royal birth, even if she was just a commoner. Clarisea was chaste and of unsurpassable beauty and had managed, he was sure, to ward off the filthy hands and lewd entreaties of successive masters, certain her lover would come to her rescue.

"There was a superior reason for my travails," Esteban says, bringing his tale to a close, his eyes alight. "This long and thin body, where my soul has been a captive, was not pure enough for her. But now, now I am worthy of Clarisea, I have been purified by these trials and tribulations, ready to bring my voyages to a felicitous conclusion. I have read in Greek novels, Byzantine novels, that true lovers can never be separated, that finally they must meet, and like those heroes, I will find her, waiting somewhere for our paths to cross again and find happiness in each other's arms."

The man is a fraud, was my first thought. And, oh dear, a buffoon, I quickly add, unable, however, to deny a certain sympathy for him, almost a baffling brotherhood between us. But there is no doubt he is mad.

Mad to think that anyone would believe a tale so lacking in verisimilitude, mad to think anyone would be taken in by all these bizarre reversals of fortune, mad to think he could fool the Inquisition and the Privy Council and the King himself, not to mention Marín and Garrido and Carrasco. And mad indeed if he didn't realize that someone like Miguel de Cervantes Saavedra, who had borne the hard chains of real captivity, would be convinced by such schemes.

And give short shrift to the man's flights of fancy, a few pointed questions would burst the bubble of his preposterous story.

Nothing of the sort. Instead, Miguel seems to be taking this liar seriously, gleaning details about the shipwreck and the pirates and in what Northern land and latitude the princess might be held, and also a philosophical question, had Esteban considered whether it was God or Lady Fortune that ruled the life of mortals?

And then my author veers in another direction, he wonders what books Esteban has been reading, if the *Aethiopica* of Heliodorus and Aquiles Tacio in the excellent translation by Nuñez de Reinoso and the answer was yes, and if Boccaccio and Bandello and the *Selva de Aventuras* by Jerónimo de Contreras and yes to that as well, and how about Apolonius of Tyre and Xenophon of Ephesus and "yes, yes, these noble books and many other romances of that variety where mishaps and troubles such as mine had been foretold, my life has been like living inside a book."

And that's when I understood, that's when it dawned and surged and shocked me that the man was indeed mad, but not because he was trying to cheat the authorities, not mad in that sense, but because . . . .

That he had gone mad from all those books, had spent his nights reading from dusk till dawn, and his nights from sunrise to sunset until he ended up believing his own lies, could it be that he needs a doctor and not a judge, that the poor delusional fellow deserves our pity rather than our derision?

What to do then with someone that sick?

Sentence him to be beaten, send him to jail? Or have him shut up forever in some cavernous building full of lunatics frothing at the mouth, condemn him to an insane asylum. An asylum! For some reason I shudder at the very name of that place where he will be mistreated and laughed at, where he will spend the rest of his days dreaming of how to rescue his nonexistent princess, reproaching himself for what she must be going through at the hands of malevolent and lascivious men, is that to be his destiny? Or would Cervantes, always affectionate, always interested in storytelling, perhaps counsel poor Esteban that if he wants to be believed, he should disguise his folly with meticulous details that sound true, if you are going to lie, best to do so persuasively.

How would I react if faced with a similar dilemma? Could I find a way to spare this man a cell from which he will never escape?

Cervantes calls for Marín, Garrido and Carrasco to enter the room. Upon seeing them, Esteban Estudillo cowers behind his protector, and whispers: "You will not forget, sir, what you swore to me in the name of the unknown lady you love?"

An imperial gesture from one of his persecutors forces the madman to leave the premises, but not before hearing my Miguel's solemn reply: "I have not forgotten. I will honor my vow to you."

The three men smile at this reassurance as Estudillo scurries away.

"So . . . do you find the defendant guilty or innocent?"

Cervantes clears his throat before saying: "Am I to understand that my decision is final and definitive, without possible appeal? That I am a real judge in this case?"

"We are your most obedient and humble servants."

"Good. Call him back in here, tell him you believe his absurd story, but that the King's treasury is depleted and he must seek relief elsewhere—it's what you say to all the former captives, the real ones, anyway. I'll give him a couple of coins so he won't go hungry, at least today."

"You haven't answered our question," Marín says. "Guilty or innocent?"

Cervantes sighs. "Gentlemen, gentlemen, would that the world and our human endeavors fit so neatly into one word like guilty, another word like innocent. Poor Estudillo is guilty because his tale is false and innocent because he does not know it is false. Just let the man be free to roam, he'll discover soon enough the difference between what is real and what is not. And anyway, who is he hurting, besides himself? People will laugh at him, true, but the world needs a little laughter. And one day he'll wake up healed of his malady, though that may well kill him. Someone so married to his mania, my guess is he'll probably die of sadness."

"And meanwhile, what? You let him go and he begins beating wayfarers up because they don't believe him, because they refuse to accept the unrivalled beauty of his false princess? Or he begs for alms from credulous churchgoers, to pay for his chimerical expedition? Insults the authorities for not coming to his aid? Think it over again, save yourself and us the trouble, Cervantes, and find him guilty once and for all."

"I don't need to think anything over. My decision will not change."

The notary intervenes, tremulously, almost pleading: "Master Cervantes, do you really want someone like this

Estudillo confusing the populace with stories of captivity that dishonor the real heroes such as yourself? And remember that it is not his fate alone that hangs in the balance, but yours as well. Are you sure that you are not making a terrible mistake?"

"A mistake would be to condemn an old man who is as crazy as he is harmless. If you force me to render a definitive decision, then I have no recourse but to find him innocent. That is my verdict."

A verdict that fills me with pride and trepidation. He is spiting powerful men. They have set up this encounter to test his loyalty and his wisdom and he is deliberately failing the test, showing them that the soldier who defied them that first time, eighteen years ago in Valencia, is still alive and kicking, that he will not play their game. Is it his arrogance, that old enemy of Miguel's, that is speaking through his mouth?

Or is it genuine compassion for that unfortunate man, is Cervantes, now that he has been given this chance, now that he has it in his power, for the first time in his existence, to save at least one person from the sort of repression he has himself suffered, recklessly determined to show mercy rather than severity? Has he not spent too many nights in dungeons, too many days listening to the stories of men and women imprisoned and threatened with violence, for him to inflict any more pain on yet another victim?

My heart also goes out to Esteban, and the closer I get to that poor maniac trapped within the confines of his own mind, the more marvelously connected I feel to Miguel de Cervantes, I rejoice that his immense generous heart is no longer separated from mine, no longer a stranger to me, and it is this deepening bond that now allows me, that is now helping me to fathom something else inside Cervantes, to see . . . .

Yes, something new and bold is indeed stirring, almost roiling, inside my author's imagination, a slight sliver of an idea that this Esteban Estudillo has slipped into Miguel. It is no more than a hint, I don't have time to examine or extend that seed or kernel or insinuation, because now Marín interrupts and intercepts my exploration, diverts Cervantes's attention, Marín lets out a laugh and the laugh is answered by one from Garrido, while Carrasco looks on glumly, the only one not to join in.

"Didn't I say it?" Marín crows. "Didn't I predict it?"

"You did, you said he'd do something rash and stupid," concedes Garrido. "*De veras te jodiste ahora,* Cervantes, you really fucked yourself up this time. And Carrasco here can't claim that we didn't bend over backwards to give you a chance."

"I bet ten *escudos* you'd prove them wrong," Carrasco says morosely. "A war hero, I said. Backed you all the way. But you failed me."

"A cripple, and blind, to boot, that's what he is. Unreliable. Sentimental. Gullible. No backbone."

"And you're going to get it right up the ass, see what happens when you flout the law."

"Gentlemen," and here Cervantes sounds genuinely puzzled by this onslaught—"you can disagree with my verdict and decide not to give me the job, but such threats, such hilarity, such vindictiveness is unwarranted, I—"

"Not give you the job? That's the least of it."

"The least of what? I considered all angles of this case, offered a solution that would injure no one."

"He still doesn't get it."

"Esteban's an actor, Miguel. Just pretending to be mad. Just challenging you to see through his performance. We didn't need you to tell us he was a fraud, which he isn't, or that he's mad, which he also isn't. You should have said: *Nice try, gentlemen. But you can't fool me, I'm not biting. Why don't you bring along someone who I can really interrogate, whose falsehoods I can really detect? Why not use me to the utmost of my abilities?*"

"Or at least, at least, at least, if you had said, *he's crazy, lock him up*, or said, *he wants to make a fool of us, lock him up ...*"

"But not even that," says Garrido. "So you're worthless to us. I was adamant that we not even trouble ourselves with procuring an actor like Sebastián Godoy, spend a day writing out lines for him to memorize. But Marín ..."

"I pointed out," Marín says, "that his services were free, this Godoy is in jail on the other side of town, at the Cárcel de la Hermandad, for assaulting who knows what group of penitents on the road to Carmona and we promised that if he managed to fool you we'd only send the bastard to the galleys and not hang him, so you've done one good deed today. C'mon, Garrido, you've got to admit that we've amused ourselves, had some good fun."

"Not that much fun for me," Carrasco laments, "having to buy ten *escudos* worth of drinks for two fellows who can gulp it down, throats as deep as the Cave of Montesinos."

"Well, that's what happens when you give undeserving people the benefit of the doubt," Marín points out. "When I was a kid, my father—"

"Enough chitchat and chitshit," Garrido says. "We have urgent business with this Miguel Cortinas or Saavedra or whatever he's calling himself now. Or are you forgetting the real reason for our visit?"

Urgent business? The real reason for this visit? Is there another surprise in store for us?

"You think I'd forget something that important?" Marín replies. "That's right, Miguel. Something we'd have had to bring up even if you'd shown yourself worthy of our trust and we'd have given you the job—because that much was true, that we need someone like you to work for us, even if you had passed the test, my man, what truly mattered was something else, what we still need to make crystal clear: your bad behavior in this jail, the reprehensible acts that we simply won't brook, not while you stay here, nor anywhere else if someday they let you go free."

I can tell that Cervantes, already stunned by the revelation that Esteban is an actor, already demoralized by how they have taken advantage of his magnanimity, is now even more dazed by this new turn of events. He says: "I don't understand."

Neither do I. I still haven't grasped what is going on. What reprehensible acts? What bad behavior?

"The *entremeses*, the little plays you staged here, Cervantes, in this very jail. We've heard about them."

"In fact, we've been reading them outside the door, while you were being hoodwinked by the *maricón* actor, making you go all mushy."

Marín waves a bunch of papers in front of Cervantes. I recognize my Miguel's convoluted, elegant handwriting. They must have raided his cell before entering the courtyard, found his work there, who knows what else?

Cervantes goes pale, falters backward a couple of steps.

"Didn't we tell you to behave, to be careful, didn't we tell you to stay out of trouble and stick to plays about captivity?"

Cervantes somehow manages to hide his anxiety, regains some boldness, and says, loud and steady: "What's wrong with my *entremeses*?"

He knows what's wrong. And so do I. I told him as he wrote them, I told him when he rehearsed them, I told him not to slot in those incendiary lines that Papa Pasamonte offered for his character, I told him, I told him, I told him to tone the silly thing down, I told him to show it first to Padre de León, but did he listen to me? Does he ever, has he ever, will he ever, listen to me?

The first interlude would have been enough to doom him, reason enough for these men or men just like them to hound him. Papa Pasamonte played Juan Paisano, an inmate awaiting a death sentence. While he and two buddies are dealing cards, the Alcaide and his notary come to confirm that Paisano is condemned to be hung for theft and murder. The prisoner acts as if he had just been delivered some flowers, suggests that they tell the judge to meet him in a field outside Sevilla and settle this whole affair, the judge with his sentence and Paisano with his dagger of *siete palmos,* and then we'll see who dies and who lives. His gambling companions persuade him, however, to appeal, perhaps the judge may be enticed to reconsider the verdict.

The card game's rowdy progress is interrupted by the whores La Beltrana and La Torbellina, who dispute Paisano's love and, more urgently, a urinal he possesses—Pasamonte insisted that nobody should doubt his prowess with women, and here the dirty jokes proliferate about what fits and doesn't fit . . . . The two *putas* lament that his enormous attributes will be lost forever to them and other worthy damsels, and Paisano says that no longer matters, all he cares about is that his face be washed after they string him up, make sure he is dressed in a nice white shirt full of starch that everyone will envy. A whole chorus of other scoundrels wander into the scene and praise Paisano for showing how a man of Sevilla dies, with his head up high, and he makes them swear that they'll stick a knife in the ribs of the snake who sentenced him. The notary rushes in to say that his sentence has been changed, thanks to La Beltrana and La Torbellina who have convinced the judge to grant clemency, *if you put in a good word for him, you can put something good and fat inside me. For each good word, two thrusts, one in and one out.* And so did the interlude conclude, with general *regocijo*, dancing and singing and verses in incomprehensible gutter slang, spectators and actors, characters and author, all mingling together on the improvised stage, celebrating Pasamonte and themselves and their irrepressible lives singing on the way to the gallows.

The second playlet, inspired by a peculiar case that Padre de León narrated to Cervantes during one of their dinners, was even more scandalous and provocative. Ten years ago, Fulano Otero, condemned to be burnt, both as a counterfeiter of royal credentials and *cédulas*, and because of accusations of sodomy, feigned insanity, forcing the authorities to delay the auto-da-fé, given that nobody can be executed without having had the chance to confess and be absolved of their sins, a confession a madman was patently unable to deliver.

The ubiquitous and histrionic Pasamonte, of course, was delighted to play the false madman with great verve and veracity, exaggerating the most disgusting comportment of the original Otero, who ate his own excrement, was tormented by lice, would let flies in and out of his mouth as if they did not bother him, all the while rocking his head back and forth, closing his eyes and emitting an incoherent babble. But once Otero's opulent brother convinced two judges—hefty bribe in hand—to transfer his relative to an insane asylum, the very next day the fake lunatic became, in De León's words, "invisible, meaning, he disappeared, and has since been sighted, very sound of mind and joyful of body, in France."

More outrageous, however, than this mockery of justice, was a phrase that Pasamonte had insisted on incorporating halfway through the interlude. When Otero's brother urged the prisoner to confess his sins secretly to a priest and repent of what he had done, in case death suddenly found him without a clean soul, Pasamonte demanded that his character respond: "I will repent of counterfeiting, but I will never repent of having loved." This, for a *pecado nefando*! And inserting, for good measure, "If I have to go to the scaffold, I would like to go hand in hand with the person I love, and not alone."

So, when the three inquisitors unexpectedly attacked the playlets he had staged, the one thing Cervantes should never have responded were the insolent words:

"What's wrong with my *entremeses*?"

They explode. That he would dare to defend his work, not show any contrition whatsoever, refuse—like his own theatrical characters—to beg forgiveness and bow his head, drives these three men into a frenzy.

"So, not only praising sodomy as love, embracing rebellion and madness, disregarding the norms of deference and civility, on top of all this, you are recalcitrant, Miguel de Cervantes, you do not seem to fully grasp what you have wrought, nor what awaits you."

"Because this is only resolved by fire, a purging of your transgressions."

I am increasingly aghast. Will they burn him, treat him like a heretic or a sodomite, like a falsifier or a murderer? My fears increase when Marín calls out in a fatigued voice, "Hey, Godoy, hey, Sebastián Godoy, you can bring it in now."

Bring what in?

Godoy enters, averting the eyes of the man he has deceived, clearly ashamed at the role he is playing in this farce—though who can tell if that is not also for show, another illusion in this world of shadows we all seem to inhabit—but what matters are not his downcast eyes or whether he is enacting remorse, what matters is that he carries a torch in his left hand and sets it down in the middle of the room.

Are they going to brand Cervantes with fire, right here, right now? No, they have other victims in mind. Garrido hands Cervantes the manuscript of the two plays.

"Burn them!"

Cervantes is startled. "You want me to . . .?"

"Burn the fuckers! Unless you'd rather we burn the hand you wrote this shit with, the hand you still use for who knows what other dirty doings?"

Cervantes hesitates, then approaches the fire with the manuscript and is about to cast it onto the flames, when

Marín says: "One by one. We want you to see each insult being engulfed by fire, each scene, each sinful bit of dialogue."

Cervantes obeys their instructions, he and I watch the pages curling up one after the other, being turned into smoke, until nothing is left of Paisano and his defiance and nothing is left of Otero and his feigned madness and even less is left of the joy with which those words, now destroyed, were created.

Cervantes still tries, nevertheless, to keep his composure. Not wanting to look at the cinders and the smoldering torch, he asks the men if that is all, he has clients to attend, your worships have had your fun and—

"Oh no, the fun has just begun," says Garrido. "You know what these are?"

And now he brings out—as if from nowhere—another bundle of papers, that I quickly recognize as something that Cervantes values far more than the two *entremeses*.

"These notes . . ." Garrido contemplates them with a mix of scorn and curiosity.

"Each one, a different case," continues Marín. "Each one, pertaining to some source that is not identified by name. Inmates, prisoners, felons. Telling you things, intimacies, ideas, broadsides, *exabruptos*, they would never tell us, not even under duress, especially under duress."

"When we discovered these, we thought, great, a treasure, we thought. But then we realized that most of these men have already been executed while some of the others, lucky bastards, were spared and are now out of reach of the law. So this information in its current form is useless to us. No need to sit down and discuss each case with you. But in the future, hey, if you have any secrets to share, we wouldn't mind taking a peek at your findings."

"When we pay you another visit, we'll see what you've flushed out from the prisoners. You could still earn some points, *hacer mérito*, get on our good side."

For once, Cervantes is prudent. He does not spit out that he is not a stoolie, that it is dishonorable to spy on friends. Instead: "I'm not writing any more letters. I'm closing that business down."

"Hey, do you think we're stupid, Miguel? If you don't write letters for these people, how will you make a living?"

"And besides, you'll want to keep talking to the prisoners, you're not one to stop. Especially because . . ."

And here Garrido grins maniacally and adds to Marín's comment: "Because these notes. You know what they look like to us? They look like sketches for a . . . what? A picaresque novel, that's what. A work that, given your obstinacy, is bound to be even more shocking than your idiotic plays."

"Those notes and sketches are not meant for any sort of fiction, gentlemen," Cervantes says weakly, "but merely ways to remember the good deeds of Padre de León and excoriate the malefactors. He's entitled to some kind of memorial and has asked me to—"

Marín looms over him.

"Do not perjure yourself, Miguel de Cervantes, on top of all your other crimes. Spies in our pay have listened in on conversations about a certain novel you are proposing to write . . . ."

Spies? What spies? How? Where?

" . . .we will not be as easily fooled by you as you have been by our actor."

"So let's do you a favor, Miguel. Just to prove how we have your best interests in sight, let's help you avoid temptation, what if we have you burn the whole lot? No need for page by page, that's how considerate we are. Come on, into the fire with them."

This time, Cervantes does not even hesitate. He chucks the notes into the blaze and, again, he and I observe how that inferno consumes his labors, all those stories and sorrows and glories, incinerates his painful and painstaking record of the men who are already dead and of women who have cried their hearts out to him, he is burning his hopes for that novel, he knows that these censors will never let it ever be published, they will keep an eye on him and, if he ever dares anything that *atrevido* and critical, they will descend upon him with their sarcasm and their torches.

But wasn't this what I wanted? That he should shunt aside these picaresque distractions and start focusing on me and my *andanzas*? Am I not to blame, in some way then, for the distress that is corroding him? Had I not prayed for some obscure deity to intervene and stop Cervantes?

And now, as if in a perverse response to those prayers, it has happened: someone—a pity it should be these repulsive men, for a terrible instant I wonder, hope that Miguel does not wonder, if Padre de León has not instigated this assault, who else could have tipped these bastards off, might he not have called them in to stop Cervantes from writing that picaresque novel, wouldn't the Padre justify his actions before God as a way of saving the soul of his friend, without realizing the consequences, these priests always think they know better than mere mortals, could it be that—but does it even matter anymore, someone, someone, someone has finally decided to knock some sense into him. Maybe the Padre is right, maybe it is time that my beloved author was taught his limits, how much, and no more, he could flaunt the mainstream beliefs of our age. For a moment, I allow myself to think that this is what he needs, allow myself to entertain the possibility that this painful experience will lead him towards enlightenment, that he can learn from it.

Quickly, however, I repent of having even abided such a thought. It is a plan that Padre de León might entertain, but not me, never me. No enlightenment, no learning, will come from this. It is enough to perceive my friend's reaction to the mortal blow these men have dealt to his plans, how they are squashing Miguel de Cervantes into the ground like a bug, down, down, down.

These men don't only own the world. They own him. And the worst is yet to come. When the fire scorches the last of the notes, Carrasco walks over to Cervantes, reaches underneath him and picks up the bag that never leaves his side. A long hand like a claw slopes into the bag and extracts . . . It is the bundle of letters.

"You boasted that you would deliver these," he says, this notary who has pretended to be kinder than his colleagues, "you asked whether I had registered your every word, swore it was your duty to bring these letters to the relatives of those captives forgotten by everybody else. You want me to read your own words back to you? How you despised us for doing our duty, promised that you would do yours? Do you remember?"

Cervantes says nothing, but yes, he remembers, of course we remember, of course he understands too late that I was right, since that night in Valencia when he subjected them to the full force of his epic dignity these rancorous scoundrels have been patiently and vindictively nursing revenge, lying in wait for the occasion to put him back in his place, teach him who has the real power, who in this world of ours has the real right to speak.

"Time to burn them as well, Miguel de Cervantes."

"Because you're too immoral to be worthy of these letters, worthy of the men who trusted you, worthy of the families that still await the news you have allowed to rot in this foul-smelling bag."

Cervantes does not resist. He does not raise his voice. He does not defend those letters with his life. He throws the whole bundle into the fire. And with each letter that burns what also burns is each promise he made in Algiers to deliver them and more recently here in this jail, what is burning is the last ember of dignity left to him, burning, burning, burning the heroic and defiant words that he recurred to in Valencia when they first interrogated him, those old words burn along with all the other words, with which he defended himself in the past and sought to defend himself today and tomorrow and will never again, after this shaming, be able to use, not those words, not any words.

It is as if they had flayed his tongue, shredded his tongue, cut off his tongue. Just when he most needs that insolent and free tongue of his, just as something had begun to cradle in his brain, just when he should be ready to write new and radiant words down, words belonging to him and no one else, composed not only for thieves and future galley slaves and counterfeiters bound for execution or slaves who have been disowned by their countrymen, not only for innocent victims of unscrupulous judges, but for everyone on this inconsolable planet spinning in space, just when the right words are shaping like ghosts in his mind, those men have left him bereft and orphaned, this time without recourse.

He watches his manhood go up in flames. He does not seem to register—or even be affected by—the final threat that one of these devils—which one? Garrido, Carrasco, Marín? Does it matter?—snakes into his ear:

"We will be watching you, Cervantes, watching you when you get out and if you get out and whether you get out, watching your every move, and every syllable you write, when and if and whether you write, we will be monitoring you closely to be sure that anything under your name or under a pseudonym conforms to good custom and doctrine, when and if and whether, whenever, wherever, whoever, always be aware of us, you don't want a third visit, that you don't want."

As the last of the letters vanishes, even the ribbon with which they were tied curling into smoke, Cervantes turns and, without uttering another syllable, walks out of that room, leaving behind the ashes of his life.

So sad, so forlorn, so defeated—my brave Miguel, my clear-eyed author, defeated?—that he does not stop at the infirmary where a host of inmates await him as they do every evening, he ignores their solicitations to come in and engage in what has been for the last four months my favorite pastime, those dreamy, pleasurable, expansive reading sessions, Miguel de Cervantes Saavedra walks by all those friends of his who have

sniffed in their nostrils the smell of his humiliation and dis-
grace, who guess from his browbeaten face that he did not
even attempt to insult his tormentors when they dishonored
him, he walks by Papa Pasamonte without saying hello or
goodbye or offering an explanation for such discourtesy or a
justification for his lack of valor, so different from what he has
learned from all of them, admired in them, he does not want
to meet their eyes.

Nor meet mine. He does not realize, as I do with mounting
anguish, that tonight of all nights would have been the perfect occasion, precisely now, for him to have finally started to
discover my existence, the moment I have been preparing for
since I emerged next to him upon his return to Spain all those
years ago, but no, he is gone, is descending the stairs and away
from his destiny, he is ruined and I am ruined with him, I am
one more of those condemned to die.

I try to enter his mind, try to give him courage, call him
back, but I am rebuffed. Shut out even from his senses, that
is how diminished he is, even his fantasies revoked, denying himself and me even a clink clink clink of hope from the
chains he has carried with him since childhood. Punishing me
as if I were the one who had created this disaster. Maybe he is
right to snub me. I have, after all, let him down.

Let him down? Is that so? Did he count on my help, really?
Has he ever attended to my advice? Does he show the faintest
sign that he appreciates that I am close by, inspiring him, urging him on, priming him for the moment of my ascendance?
Or are all my efforts a mere illusion, similar to the one that has
just been stripped from Cervantes? Have I been comforting
myself, as the muses do, as men and women when they are

no more than fetuses and phantoms in the womb, with the thought that I am in some way responsible for my own existence, pretend that I have some measure of control over the plot that will be granted to me? But this is who I am. Like all those of my kind—I do not know them, have not encountered any yet, hope to do so if ever I get to journey at last on my own road—I cannot live without that illusion, without the hope, fictitious as it may be, that I can penetrate and divine the ultimate enigma of creation, how someone like me is born.

This is how I am, who I am, but Miguel de Cervantes does not acknowledge it, does not turn to me. Once in the cell, he gets down on his knees and prays to someone else, faraway, who cannot help him as I could.

I do not know what words he utters inside or even if there remain any words at all within reach, but from the abrupt way he stands up without bothering to brush the dirt away, it is clear that Christ has not answered him and the Virgin has not answered him and Heaven has not answered, not even the fiends of Hell are interested in responding to his pleas for guidance.

Only I am here in his hour of need and I have never felt more distant.

Only I am here and I have never felt farther from being born.

SIX

" . . . In the margins of this great history were written these very comments: *'I cannot comprehend and cannot persuade myself that everything written in this chapter actually and punctually happened. The reason is that all the adventures up to this point have been possible and plausible, but with regard to this one . . . I can find no entry point that allows me to consider it true since it goes far beyond reasonable limits . . . You, reader, since you are a prudent person, judge it according to your own fancy, for I must not and cannot do more.'"*

—*Don Quixote de la Mancha*

THE RESURRECTION STARTS the next morning. I have kept watch over him all night. He does not sleep, does not toss, does not turn, does nothing in fact but stare into the darkness and listen to the breathing and belches and grunts of his fellow prisoners.

When dawn filters into that chamber, his eyes close as if he is unwilling to let light bless him in any form, his eyes close and sleep comes for him, and also, for the first time in these eighteen years, for me. Along with him I must have fallen into a deep pit of dreamlessness—it was like death, that slumber, without the restful reminiscence of even an image to accompany me when I awake with Miguel as a hand shakes his shoulder, reverently, more of a touch than a shake, and my eyes and his open to see that the other inhabitants of the cell have left, filed out who knows how long ago towards the gloom of the corridors, the other cells, the central courtyard, none of them

disturbing his sleep, none of them having urgent affairs to settle with him as Josep Jordán does.

Jordán is an old *alcahuete*, his beard flowing down to his
waist, white and grubby. "Beg your pardon for waking you,
sir," he says now apologetically, "but I was wondering about
my letters. You never showed up yesterday, sir, disappeared
with those three devils and I—"

"You have paid for them, of course," Miguel says, standing up resignedly. He reaches into a crevice in the wall and
extracts the pimp's two letters, sighs with relief: they were not
confiscated, not burnt. He adjusts his broken glasses and reads
the correspondence to Josep.

One is a statement to the court concerning the general
need for pimps. It was not a difficult argument to make, that
pimps should not be jailed but rather commended, as they are
a necessity for the peace and pleasure of the kingdom. The old
man likes it, the fancy words, the quotations from Aristotle
and Ariosto and Cicero and the Bible. And, as for the second
assignment, he is even more impressed with the petition to
the judges begging for mercy, the allusions to his advanced age
and time spent as a soldier in Italy, his many acts of repentance
that Padre de León can attest to.

Impressed and yet slightly dubious: "You think they will
show mercy, do you, do you, good sir?"

I can tell that Cervantes only wants to be left alone forever
without having to engage this old man or anyone else on this
earth, not now, not ever, but he is Cervantes, he will always
respond when someone is in need, that is simply his nature.

"Josep, Josep," he says, trying to hide his weariness, "What
matters is not if you are right or wrong, guilty or innocent, but

that they should find a reason to make an exception. This letter should soften the heart of the most obdurate judges. Let us hope it brings you luck. It is, after all, the last one I will ever write."

"What about the lady?"

"What lady?"

"A lady who came in to visit you and ask for your help, after you were—well, escorted away yesterday. She waited until closing bells rang and is back early this morning, first one in line downstairs, in front of your table."

"Tell her the business is closed."

"She's a pretty lass. Not that I've seen her face even. Veiled, she is. But I have not made a decent living out of women without having developed a sniff for certain hidden virtues. If her face is anything like her hands and what her bird-like voice promises, she may well be deemed the most beautiful of all the women in Sevilla and maybe of this realm. I'd give her a chance, sir. She requested that I tell you that some good might come of your encounter with her."

"Some good," snorts Cervantes. "Me? Do some good? Receive some good? Tell her to go away."

"If that is what you command, sir. But she has the stubborn air of someone who will return day after day until you agree to meet. As to doing good, she added something that I didn't quite comprehend, and when I asked her what that meant, she said to repeat it to you, word for word. *Tell him: Is there any reward for goodness except the chance to do more good?*"

Cervantes is startled, repeats the words, as if to himself, as if from long ago: "Is there any reward for goodness except the chance to do more good?"

"The very words."

He does not want, as I do not want, to lend credence to the thought that has crept into his head. And yet, he does, he has to, he cannot ignore that message, its effect so strong that the curtains of darkness and silence he drew around himself last night begin to sweep away and I am able to start peering into him again, gradually gaining access to his thoughts.

"How old is this woman?"

"By her voice and her hands and the lithesome way she moves, I'd say in her early or mid twenties."

"Not older?"

"I know something about age and women, sir. Definitely in her prime."

Suddenly energized and curious, Cervantes says, "Tell her I will be down soon."

And, even so, as he pisses in a bucket and then changes his shirt, combs his beard, washes his face, I can notice him becoming wary, yesterday's lesson of mistrust and degradation crawling back into his soul.

Cautious, I whisper to him, yes, we need to be cautious. But a few minutes later, as he descends the stairs, before he even glimpses the lady who has sent him those words pronounced in Algiers, his wariness dissipates as an aroma tickles his nostrils, and mine, and mine. It's a soft smell that floats slightly above the smell of the jail, somehow apart, somehow uncontaminated by the stench of vomit and spit and congealed blood from the latest brawl, the sharp pungent jasmine that he last breathed into his lungs all those years ago on that return to Algiers to bring Zahara back with him, the fragrance of soap with which she graced the tiny curve behind her ears.

To him, therefore, when he does see the woman waiting in the courtyard, it is as if she materializes out of the scent itself, seems to embody it, her perfume gets stronger as she turns, appears to recognize him the more she advances with each step, dainty and nervous and energetic. And he finds himself without defenses as her fluttering veil flows towards him, he is overwhelmed, he—

And composes himself, determined not to be ruled by a riot of emotions, has learned enough about life to realize that if he wishes to control this situation—who is she? Why has she come? Could she, could she possibly . . .?—he needs to find out as much as he can about this mysterious petitioner without revealing his own puzzlement and expectations, not let the wafting smell of that soap disarm him.

She stops in front of my Miguel.

Water, I think, and he does too, she reminds us of water on a hot day, even the way she bows slightly, like a quiet cascade.

"Miguel de Cervantes."

It is not a question. More of an affirmation, a confirmation, a definition. Of him, yes, but also of her, because the accent in Spanish has the inconsequential, throaty, guttural inflection of someone versed in Arabic, again, again, like Zahara, first the perfume and then this, as if he were being visited by an apparition from the past and not someone of flesh and blood.

"At last," she says.

"I am sorry you had to wait, Señora," he says, choosing each word carefully. "Yesterday was not the most propitious day to greet you. At times, angels come to see me from beyond these barriers. Yesterday, it was the turn of the demons."

"I was not referring to yesterday, sir. Or this morning. My wait has been for far longer than a day. Ever since—" She does not complete the thought, hesitates, decides to veer off in a different direction. "We have—my husband and I—need of your services."

"The shop is closed, Señora . . . I'm afraid I'm no longer in that business, not anymore."

"Afraid? Not you. Not Miguel de Cervantes."

For a second, I am amused, though Cervantes does not smile. Her proclamation is so childish, so innocent, reverberates with such awe, how can he not be charmed? And then I realize where his guardedness comes from. Could she not be another fraudulent performer out to fool him? If those hellhounds are seeking to trap him yet again, would they not choose precisely someone like this damsel in distress, would they not have told her to wear a veil to pique his interest and vanity, found out through who knows what devilish pact with memory that a certain phrase from the past would entice him into making yet another mistake, that a certain perfume would render him defenseless?

"Only a madman does not know fear."

"But not you, never you, Miguel de Cervantes." It comes pouring out of her like the surge of the sea, he suddenly remembers how the waves hit the beach near the garden, where he first met Juan, last saw Juan executed, why does he now recall the merciless, yet hopeful sea of Algiers? "The stories—they still speak of you back there, from where we have just, my husband and I, escaped a mere three months ago, but so many years listening to what you had done, how you took the blame over and over again, how you faced down the King, how you saved the others, almost all of them, almost . . . —" Again, she stops, this time at that word, almost, *casi*, why not all, all? But she resumes: "I was brought up on stories of a man who was fearless, told by so many, but especially by my lady."

Her lady? Her lady? Cervantes does not want to acknowledge what he is grasping at, the question he dares not formulate but that is already shaping in his mind and has definitely surfaced into mine.

"That fearless man is dead, Señora. He cannot help himself, let alone you, you and your husband."

"I don't believe you."

"Forgive me for being candid, but I am the one who has reason not to believe you. Someone hidden behind a veil, when here am I, right here, exposed to your scrutiny?"

"So, for you to consider my plea that you tell our story as you have done for others with such success, I must show my face?"

"Unless you do so, this conversation is over."

He recognizes her at once. Even if the only time he has seen her it was dark and she was perhaps five years old and sleeping and those eyes that are now revealed to him like the first light of dawn were then closed, even so, he knows immediately, as soon as she casts aside the veil. He tells himself that he doesn't need to trace the contours of the cheekbones of her father, those are the selfsame lips that Juan used to perpetually smile and whistle with—what's this? Juan? Juan the gardener, Juan Navarra is her father?—unmistakably his daughter.

Does she know that Miguel once watched her curled up in that bed in the room Zahara guided him towards, shushing him as they tiptoed in and slipped out again after several minutes in her quiet, breathing company, is there anything more lovely than a child that dreams the night away, a child that does not know what awaits her, does not know that many years will pass before the eyes she did not feel examining her in the deep dusk of Algiers once more will alight on her skin, her brows, her hair, her own eyes? Does she know who Cervantes really is? What sacrifice conjoins him to her dead father? And Zahara, what of Zahara? How can this be happening to him now, precisely now that he is so desperate and inarticulate and betrayed?

How to react? Say: *Cristina.* Say: *your lady, what is your lady's name?* Say: *Juan.* Say: *what is your plan, why have you come?* Say: *I am glad you have come, I am glad you are alive, I am glad that we can speak.*

Or better wait. If this is a game—and why else would she not have told him from the start who she was, who had sent her, what happened to Zahara?—if she is indeed playing at something, hiding something—no, it cannot be a trap, at least not set by those men, they have no idea of the existence of this woman who was once a little girl, the memory of Zahara that he has kept from everybody on this earth except me—if it is true that she has come to ask for help, then let her do so, let her take the first and the second step and the next ones as well, he needs time to figure this out, figure out what he is feeling, he likes what is rising and unfolding inside him too much, the suspicion of adventure and unpredictability, he likes it too much for his own good, better not to ask the question that is burning inside him, better to wait.

"And now that you have seen my face, sir, will you help our cause?"

"Why me?"

"Before I left Algiers, my lady told me that if I was in trouble I should come to you. A man, she said, who knows that goodness and beauty merge into the same word, *ihsan*."

"Ah, the Koran."

"I was told by her that you took your wisdom from wherever you could find it. That I could trust your goodness and talent. That is what my lady said."

And now he cannot stop himself, I don't wish to restrict him either, I am also anxious for the answer.

"Your lady?" Miguel de Cervantes says. "Who is this lady you keep referring to?"

"Zahara."

The name comes out clear as a trill in the murky air of this prison and then the same name is repeated again, haltingly, "Zahara," and then again, over and over until those syllables become sobs, and that is how Cervantes, before Cristina can tell him that it is so, discovers that Zahara is dead.

As the sobs dwindle and turn back into words, the story she wishes him to write for her gradually begins to emerge.

"Like my dead lady, I was born in Spain and brought into captivity as a baby. And like you, I owe everything to her."

Cervantes is about to ask something and then decides—he who has had to learn patience—that this tale will admit no interruptions.

"I was born in Navarra," Cristina continues. "but it was our misfortune that my father was offered work as a gardener in Playa del Rey. I don't know if you have ever been there or heard of it, a small town south of Valencia where my mother is buried and where I shall journey with my husband once our case has been resolved. She was killed by renegades and Moors when they raided us, carried my father and me away. Of her I have no memories. Of him, of Juan Navarra, only a song:

> *De laurel*
> *es la rama,*
> *de verde laurel,*
> *de laurel siempre verde*
> *como mi querer,*
> *la rama del laurel,*
> *prisionerito*
> *mi amante en Argel,*
> *¡Jesús qué dolor!*
> *prisionerito,*
> *cautivo está mi amor.*

"He would come and sing it outside the house into which I was sold, *From laurel is the branch, from green laurel, evergreen laurel, like my love, a helpless prisoner.* I don't know how he managed to find out where it was or how he convinced his owner to allow him to roam our street, perhaps that infidel Agi Morato worried that if his gardener was not content the fruit in the orchards would sour, or perhaps he simply understood the sorrow of losing a daughter, though I am not sure if that man had any heart at all, given what he did later. But at least Morato's indulgence made it possible for me to keep that one memory of my father, not knowing at the time that he was the singer, not knowing that it was Juan who was sending me that music and those words, *a helpless prisoner, my love in Argel, oh Jesus, such pain, a helpless prisoner, my captive love.* Nevertheless,

I must have recognized something in them as I repeated that song so often to myself that I was able to teach it to my lady Zahara when she had her husband buy me from the corsair who was my owner. Only later, much later, when I was told who my father had been and how he had died and why, only then did I understand how much he had loved me, only then did I identify the song with his voice, his voice with my life."

Cristina stops and sighs, and Cervantes searches for some reproach in her tone, the possibility that she knows that Juan was murdered because of his friendship with the man sitting in front of her in this Sevilla jail, but—as if she could read his mind with the ease that I now can—she smiles at him reassuringly and accepts the hand he reaches across the table, accepts the soft trace of that consolation. And only recommences her tale when he withdraws his fingers.

"I suppose I always had the hope, as a child, that my father would come for me, that vague, hazy sense that I, like other youngsters, had a father, but the one who came was my lady Zahara. She incorporated me into her household, brought me up as a Christian, just as secretly as she had been by her own mother, and part of our secret was that one day I would escape, she would find a way to send me back to the Spain where I had been born, so I could practice my faith openly, the journey home she had refused to take. I think that is why, once I arrived at puberty, she kept me apart from her son Jamaal, my dearest childhood friend. She must have been afraid we would fall in love, that he might leave Algiers with me or I might stay forever. And perhaps she even saw something dangerously incestuous in our attraction to each other, that her son and the girl she brought up as the daughter she never had, that we should . . . . So she kept me far from him and close to herself, by her side day and night.

"Indeed, my lady loved me so dearly that she could not imagine me ever being separated from her, not by a room even, let alone the wide Mediterranean Sea. And thus, the years passed without her setting those escape plans in motion. And I believe that she would not have done so, if she had not realized she was ill and that if she did not act soon, I would be entombed in Algiers for the rest of my life. At least that is what I have since deduced, because she did not confide in me immediately that she was sick, simply told me one day that the moment had come, that she had some ideas about how to accomplish the getaway she had been talking about for so long. It took, in any case, great cunning and carefulness on her part, because her husband had retired from piracy and become more jealous with every hour that passed, she was not as free as when you were held hostage there, sir.

"Next to our palace there was a house where many captives were imprisoned, a *bagno*, we called it, and the enclosed terrace where some of these men would spend time was just below one of our *ventanillas*, so we could observe them, unaware, through the slatted, interlaced *celosías* of our small windows.

"*Look at these men judiciously, do not let your sight be dimmed. One of them will lead you to freedom, you will choose him as your husband before you have ever touched his hand or he has seen your countenance. Heaven and the Holy Mother, Lela Marien, will guide you wisely.* And so I spent mornings and often afternoons examining those Christian *cautivos* until I finally settled upon one of them, perhaps less handsome than others, perhaps not as well dressed, but the way he made the company laugh, the upright bearing, the confidence in his stride, the reserve he often displayed without lapsing into melancholy, the dignity with which he responded to his master's questions or recriminations, the loving diligence with which he attended to the sorrows of his fellows when they pined for home and healed their bruises and lacerations after they had been beaten, convinced me that he could both be trusted and would be a perfect companion on the road ahead—and the stormy seas.

"Approving of my choice, my lady Zahara sent a eunuch dwarf in whom she put all her trust to find out about this man's lineage and whether he had been steadfast under duress and what others thought of him. All the reports that came back were superb: Francisco Ahumada—for such was my future husband's name—had been born in the mountains of León, of noble parentage, bred by a profligate father who had died without leaving a penny to his son, forcing the lad to become a soldier, and so valiant that it took forty Berbers to overcome him in a battle near the coast of Algiers. And he had never renounced his faith nor denounced any other captive in order to cultivate favor with the powerful, and everybody spoke of his modest temperament and agreeable disposition. Everybody, save a cleric, Juan Blanco de Paz, who had been circulating dreadful rumors about him."

Cristina stopped. She had noted, as had I, that something was troubling Cervantes. Looking inside him, I understood the reason: Juan Blanco de Paz. That was the very name of one of his fellow *cautivos*, also a cleric, who had denounced and betrayed him. Could it be a mere coincidence? Or was the same malevolent friar still plotting deviously against his countrymen, trying to curry favor with his Muslim superiors? All these years later? Impossible, as that iniquitous man had been ransomed, returned to Spain and had given up the ghost four years ago in Baza, under the shadow of the Jabalcón mountain in Granada.

"It's nothing," Miguel says now. "Not to worry."

"Not to worry," agreed Cristina. "Just what our eunuch said. *Not to worry,* he told his lady Zahara, *this cleric is a fraud, has falsely suggested he is an official of the Holy Inquisition, is known as envious and full of villainy, and his accusations stem from having been excluded from a previous attempt by Ahumada to escape, and should be taken, rather, as one more piece of evidence that we have chosen wisely, that we can entrust this man with the life of your Cristina.*

"And so my lady proceeded to contact Francisco Ahumada. The way in which this occurred is one of the reasons why here in Spain they so consistently disbelieve our story. My benefactress wrote a letter to him, and attached it to a pole, along with a pouch full of valuable coins. She and I poked that pole through one of the apertures of our *ventanilla*, letting it down onto the terrace level. And the hostages, one by one, approached our offering and, one by one, we lifted the pole upwards and then from side to side, as if to say, no, no, no, this is not for you, until Francisco's turn came and we let him receive our message and coins. The letter explained that there was a young slave woman in the palace next door, clandestinely devoted to Christ and his Mother, Lela Marien, and desirous of leaving Algiers with someone she could tender her life to. If he was willing to risk everything and swore to marry her as soon as they arrived in Spain, fortune would smile upon him.

"His answer came soon enough, two days later when the hostages were on the terrace without any guards to detect their actions. Francisco got down on his knees, bowed to the ground, as if praying, looked up towards our window and showed a piece of paper in his hand. I lowered and manipulated the pole so it was ready to receive his message.

"Which was a declaration of love and devotedness so plainly felt and eloquently manifested, that both my mistress and I were overcome with joy. This time, I answered personally, detailing our plan and adding four thousand *doblas* to ransom Ahumada himself and those companions he could bank on, as long as he made sure they were also strong oarsmen. If he consented to set this part of the strategy up, someone of our entire confidence—we did not reveal it was the eunuch dwarf—would purchase a *bajel* and provision it, readied by a renegade from Asturias who wished to return to the fold of Christ and to his aging parents before they died without having said their farewells.

"As letters came and went, and our conspiracy progressed, each step more perilous, each step bringing us closer to our goal, my lady, realizing that she was ailing faster than expected, decided to take me into her confidence. She had not much longer to live, she said, but wished to use this adversity to further our plans. She asked her husband to arrange for her to spend her last days in the palace and gardens of Agi Morato, next to the sea, those groves she had always loved, happiest when she was plucking jasmine flowers and herbs for her soap. He agreed, of course, comprehended that she wanted to die peacefully close to him and their son, and naturally did not object to her entourage accompanying her, meaning myself and the eunuch.

"*We'll be right next to where the ship will land to free you and your future husband and his mates,* she said. *I want our last moments together to be in that garden where I met your father, where your father befriended Miguel de Cervantes, where your father sang his song of laurel and greenery and love and loss, the garden where your father died, I want him to be present as you leave this land and I leave this world. I have not found his bones or his ashes, no matter how much I have looked—be sure to tell Cervantes this when you see him, wherever that brave man may now be. Tell him that I said that Juan's spirit is still in that garden and that it will find rest when it sees his daughter on her way home. Oh my dear Cristina, your father will surely bless you from heaven and make your journey safe.*

"And we would, in effect, be many times in need of Juan Navarra's blessing, sooner than we had assumed—because disaster struck us even before our departure from Algiers.

"The night we were to embark, my lady took a sudden turn for the worse and was thus unable, as she had desired, to bid goodbye to me in the garden, nor even meet my savior Francisco face to face. Behind the closed doors of her chamber in Agi Morato's mansion by the sea, after we had cried more tears than could fill an ocean, she asked me to dress in one of her most lavish Moorish robes and decked me up with all the jewelry she possessed, diamonds and bracelets and pearls, and then handed me a coffer, full of gold *doblas*.

"*This is your dowry,* she said. *It will make things easier for you in your new life, because if you lack money all sorts of other miseries will follow.* And then added after a meditative pause: *Do you know what my Cervantes used to say: He who loses wealth, loses much; he who loses friends, loses more; but he who loses courage, loses all. And so, Cristina, if you should find yourself without this coffer to protect you, remember you will always have me as a friend, carry me with you—and above, all courage, as Cervantes once told me. Cervantes, Cervantes. When you see him, he will ask if, at the end, I had some final message for him. I have told you often what I said to him when we parted, the one word I left him with. Write, I said. But I have not heard from the new captives who arrive daily on our shores of anything memorable he has composed, and so perhaps he could use some more advice, another sort of command. Tell him,*—and this she whispered in my ear, so low I could hardly hear, and yet hear it I did—*tell him to write as if he were already dead, because the dead always tell the truth, the dead have nothing to fear. Tell him that.*"

Cristina pauses here and looks at Cervantes, awaits a reaction, gets none, says: "The last words she ever spoke."

He cannot tell her that he had reached the decision, just the night before, to never write again, he cannot tell her that his courage had failed him, he cannot tell her that Zahara's words are both a slap in the face and also an incitement to become the man he once was and perhaps still can be. Is it possible that now, precisely now, God has sent him this girl, how to make sense of this coincidence, this accident of fortune?

He searches for something to say, mechanically comes up with: "The last words she ever spoke?" as he slowly, deliberately, painfully, thinks of Zahara in her last bed, wonders whether Zahara faced Spain or somewhere else as she died.

"Yes," Cristina answers. "Because then she closed her eyes and waved weakly towards the door, and I obeyed her, what else could I do? And before I could realize what was happening,

I was in the garden and there he was, my Francisco, the eunuch had opened the gate for him and his companions, there he was, the man we had chosen to be my liberator. And he was radiant under the moon that my father had so often admired, and I lifted my veil as I did for you, dear sir, so he could see the face and guess the body of the woman he had betrothed. And our eyes met in the shadows and we knew neither of us had made a mistake and he took me in his arms and then . . . .

"Jamaal, sweet Jamaal, my darling boy and playmate, the son of the lady I owed my life and my religion and my future to, Jamaal chanced into the garden, crying because of his mother. The moonlight caught the glint of his tears and must have blurred his vision because he was unprepared when a group of the fugitives, hovering by the gate, rushed towards him, grabbed his arms, pinning him down, so surprised that all he could manage was to croak *Christians! Christians! Thieves!*, because his captors swiftly stuffed a rag in his mouth, dragging him out of the garden to the nearby beach where our narrow vessel was already set to sail.

"The moon shone stronger there, with no trees or shadows to obstruct Jamaal's view, so when he remarked me and the eunuch among the Christians, he began to struggle with more ferocity than before, presuming that I had been kidnapped along with his mother's trusted servant. A quick blow to the head knocked Jamaal out.

"And suddenly, all was silent. But not for long. A chaotic chorus of opinions erupted. Most of those men, consumed by hatred and fear, wanted to kill him right away. I pleaded for his life—he was my brother, the son of the woman who had made our escape possible. Some then suggested tying him up and leaving him on the beach, a solution that the renegade refused to entertain: Jamaal would soon be found and we would be pursued and caught. *Take him with us then*, Francisco said, with authority. *Quick, every minute that passes we are in more danger.* I was still not satisfied: *And then what? What will you do with him?*

"*I promise, on my honor, that no harm will come to this young man who, through no fault of his own, is now our captive as we were once recently the captives of his people.*

"And with this assurance, Jamaal was carried onto the boat and we embarked, soundlessly rowing out into the bay. I was terribly upset. Jamaal had become a victim of my search for freedom and his mother was dying right now without her son by her side, without him when she most needed him. Would she bitterly realize that his absence was due to her attempt to save me? My despair was so implacable that I hardly had the presence of mind to savor the first minutes of that freedom, did not fully enjoy the farewell my body was saying to the life I had led in Algiers, barely perceived how the shore and the garden beyond it were receding into the distance as if they were phantoms, as if none of this could possibly be happening. A dream, a dream, I thought, all this must have been dreamt by someone else.

"I watched until I could no longer distinguish the trees or the mountains or the dim lights of the mansion where my lady was also saying goodbye to her life, but her life was ending as mine was beginning, and only then, nestled in the arms of my bridegroom, did I turn and face the sea we had yet to cross if we were to be safe.

"And found Jamaal staring at me from the bow of our small ship. Staring at me, who knows for how long he had been staring at me in the embrace of Francisco, staring at the rich clothes that belonged to his mother, staring at the necklaces of his mother that I was wearing and her bracelets and rings and a lovely anklet on my left foot, staring at the coffer at my side, recognizing the coffer, understanding that I was part of the conspiracy, that I had betrayed him and—how could he think otherwise?—betrayed my lady Zahara.

"*Jamaal,* I called out to him, *Jamaal, dearest brother Jamaal, it's not what you—*"

"But he didn't hear the rest of what was supposed to be an explanation, my plea. Roaring like a wounded animal, he threw himself overboard, into the churning sea—and would have drowned if Francisco had not leapt in after him and, with the help of several mates, brought him safely back on board.

"Jamaal was spluttering water but more than water: curses, lamentations, loathing, venom, profanities, more and more as I tried to calm him down, begged him to trust that the Holy Virgin, Lela Marien, would take care of him. But he did not cease his tirade until again a rag closed his mouth, and only stopped gesticulating obscenely once they tied his hands behind his back.

"*This one's got a lot of strength,* the renegade observed. *He'll fetch us a good price when we reach land, Spain, Sicily, Malta, wherever. Unless,* he said to me unpleasantly, *you can convince him to convert.*

"I was about to answer that I would not allow my friend, not this man or any other man or woman or child, to be made a slave, when Francisco intervened: *There is a beach East of here, at Sargel which I know well from when I was part of the expedition from Orán that led to my capture. It is isolated from human habitation, so we can leave him there without jeopardizing his future or ours.*

"He pronounced these words with such certainty and command, that no one dared to contradict him, though I saw several of the men exchange dark glances with the renegade, concerned that we were putting our whole enterprise at risk by returning to the very Africa they—and we—had been trying to escape. And for a Muslim infidel!

"I try to assuage my regret now, all these months later, by remembering that this good deed proved my lover's virtuous heart, but I still hear the screams of Jamaal from the shore when he was deposited there, I cannot forget how he tore his hair and his beard, his curses upon me for having deceived and fleeced the family that had given me refuge, he called me whore and plunderer, *nahib* and *sarraq*, and murderer of his mother, *did you poison her, you puta, sarmuta, mumis, ahira, did you plan it so I would not be there when she died, do you hate us so much, slut, thief, liar, may Allah punish you, may Allah sink your ship and drown you, and watch the fish eat you before carting your carcass off to Hell*, and then, at the very end, *come back, Cristina, come back and all is forgiven, I have always loved you*, and then, *may your children be born with deformities and blind and die of the black plague, may you hear my voice in your ears forever cursing*, and then his voice grew fainter and the sound of the waves took over and the soothing words of Francisco lapped into me as we headed northwards.

"If Jamaal's curses had been limited to disturbing my mind, then . . . but no, the sea seemed to hear them and the wind, the tramontane and the waves were responding to Jamaal's fury, listening to him still, and God must have been listening too, because a storm was brewing, descending upon us with all the wrath of nature, all the anger of Jamaal. We tried to outrace it, the men rowing with all their might and into the dawn as the dark clouds advanced howling upon our skiff—and I thought, if I could stop Jamaal's words from coursing through me the rage of the waters would subside, it was all my fault, that's what I thought, that's what I still think.

"I do not need to describe to you, Miguel de Cervantes, what a storm at sea can do to our frail ships and even frailer bodies, you know what it is like when a ship begins to sink, when the men cry out as wave after gigantic wave begins to claim them.

"But my father's blessings were still with us, and the love of my lady Zahara, and our Sweet Lord Jesus did not forsake us, at least not my future husband and me. He was a strong swimmer and a sturdy soul and, grabbing me with one arm and a large floating board from the wreckage with the other, he managed to keep us alive long enough for the wind to subside and another coast to appear before our eyes, until we finally staggered ashore, more dead than alive, in Vélez de Málaga.

"The rest of the crew, the renegade, the eunuch dwarf, must have perished—as we have had no notice that any of them survived. It pains me to think of them sleeping at the bottom of the sea, along with the coffer and all its gold. Fortunately, we still had the jewels I was wearing, which stood us in good stead.

"Because we were not greeted with roses and compassion. The Spanish guard, alerted by a goatherd who ran in panic from us when he saw my Moorish robes, were suspicious for the same reason; they did not like my accent, nor believed Francisco's story, saying they had just been fooled but a few months ago by someone just like him claiming to be an escaped slave who had turned out to be a spy and a terrorist and a thief, the scout for a raid that was repulsed though not before several townspeople had been kidnapped. And things got worse when three men arrived—three horrible men, two interrogators and their notary, with nasty questions and obscene insinuations. Somehow they had got their hands on a report sent by that cleric Juan Blanco de Paz, they enjoyed reading the accusations against Francisco over and over again.

"*Prove they are false!* And Francisco couldn't, though he had prepared for precisely that sort of situation. Knowing that Juan Blanco de Paz was determined to ruin his reputation, my future husband had gathered an *información*, a series of sworn statements from twenty-four witnesses in Algiers, noble and forthright hostages who could vouch for Francisco's valor and faith and excellent customs, testimonies that had been duly certified by a notary, himself a captive.

"Proof that had sunk, along with the ship and our companions and the coffer. But there was one thing that did not sink or disappear—and that was the hope in you, Miguel de Cervantes, the memory I held fiercely inside me and the message sent by my lady Zahara, the certainty that you would be there to assist me in the name of my father, the memory of what my father offered you as his farewell, as if he were saying goodbye to me. That's what I evoked at the worst moments, even when those men threatened me, especially when those men promised to save me if I denounced Ahumada as a fraud, if I corroborated the charges of his enemy, at the moments of most disarray, I remembered how my father had gone through something far more terrible and yet, and yet, he winked."

Here she is interrupted by Cervantes, who rises from his seat, totters and then falls back onto the rickety chair.

"Is something wrong? Are you well, dear sir?"

"How did you know that? That he winked? Your father?"

Cristina's voice is serene and clear. "My lady Zahara told me, who else?"

Cervantes is shaken. He never told Zahara, he never told anybody about that wink, never revealed it to me either. Only now, only at this instant in which Cristina reminds him of that signal, only now am I allowed access to that moment in his past, seeing for the first time the execution of Juan Navarra.

This is what I witness. How Cervantes, relieved that he hasn't been slain for hiding in that cave next to the garden during his escape, thankful that Zahara had managed to get her husband to intervene and save his life, does not immediately realize why he is being marched by four janissaries outside the gates of Algiers to the very garden where he found his friend Juan already on a scaffold, hanging from both his arms, ready to be martyred by a group of soldiers under the command of Agi Morato. Because if the Moors have to choose between killing a poor gardener who nobody would pay a cent for and this Spaniard with letters from the brother of the King, there was no doubt who would die. What mattered was less to kill Juan—that was incidental, an insignificant corollary, the disappearance and suffering of someone expendable— than to impart an exemplary lesson for the witness, a message to Cervantes: look at what you have ended up doing to this simple man who believed in your words, look at the consequences of your action, look on this death and shudder. It was a performance of pain, meant to turn the lion into a lamb and forever paralyze the witness with terror.

What those men did not realize was that Juan would not collaborate in this drama, that even in his death he was not willing to succumb to the role his captors had written out for him.

I watch through the mind of Cervantes, I watch Juan, round-bellied and stocky, hanging in the air, battered and brutalized, and his face bruised so badly that one of the eyes is swollen and unable to move or see, I am there at the moment when Cervantes is silently asking for his forgiveness, one word from Juan, a word that cannot come because his tongue has been cut out. That mouth, that mouth that had once spouted proverbs and folk wisdom as if from a fountain!

It would have been easy to despair on that occasion, just as Cervantes had lost all hope yesterday when he was taunted and disgraced by those three men, but Juan back then offered his friend an entirely different outcome, Juan transformed that terrifying moment of his execution into an act of defiance, he would not let these people have the last word.

I watch as if I were there, entirely present. Juan looks at Cervantes with his one good eye and, just before he is strangled, Juan Navarra winks, and then, to make sure Miguel knows it is no accident, that this is a deliberate gesture, his spirit unbroken, he again opens and closes that one eye of his playfully, Juan tells Cervantes not to lose courage or faith, *live for me, my friend, and live plentifully, and make others laugh and remember me and this wink*, that is the last thing Juan Navarra does on this earth of ours.

And looking inside Cervantes I can also confirm that he has never told anybody, not even Zahara, about that benediction. So how can she have told it to Cristina, how can Cristina know it? It is not the only inconsistency in the story of captivity he has just heard.

Even as he was entranced by that tale, finding it oddly familiar, strangely recognizable, too many questions kept surfacing. How did the eunuch manage to buy a boat without all of Algiers gossiping about it, without his master and the master's son Jamaal finding out? And who was this nameless renegade who had offered to be captain of that ship, how had Zahara been in touch with such a man if her husband had become so jealous? And that enigmatic husband, where was he on the night Zahara was dying? Would he have left her alone, given her so much time to dress her slave and shower her with jewelry? Were there no guards in Agi Morato's garden, at that beach? And this Agi Morato, was it possible that the same old infidel who had once owned Juan was still around? As to Francisco Ahumada, how had he accounted for abruptly coming into possession of money enough to ransom himself and the other hostages? Had he feigned that a merchant like Onofre Exarque had provided the funds? How strange to use that pole or rod to communicate with the captives, such a contrived method when it would have made more sense and been less perilous for this ubiquitous eunuch to deliver the message in person. No wonder those bastard interrogators were suspicious, found the story fantastical and dubious, preferred to give credence to the malicious allegations of Juan Blanco de Paz—and how could it be that Ahumada's accuser had the same name as the cleric who had persecuted Cervantes all those years ago, how could it be that Ahumada had protected himself against that sort of malevolence by collecting, again like Cervantes, exactly twenty-four eyewitness reports from fellow hostages to vouch for his honesty? And why did Zahara never mention Alicax, the Moor whose remains she had sworn to find, why was Alicax, that other executed and loyal friend of his, absent from this tale?

And then there was the perfume, what most disturbed Cervantes was the aroma of Zahara's soap, still surrounding Cristina in spite of the months that had passed since her escape. As to Cristina and her religiosity, she has spoken often of the Blessed Virgin, calling her Lela Marien, but not once of attending mass, entering a church with the prospect of taking holy communion, not once of confession as a way of doing penance.

And yet, Cervantes is reluctant to question her further, to play the part of one of those three men who have tormented her, suspiciously similar to the trio that has made his own life miserable. There had to be an explanation for each of his quibbles: Maybe Cristina knew the formula for that soap of Zahara's and made it here in Spain? Maybe Zahara's husband had been away on urgent business thinking his wife had still many days left? Maybe this young lady believes, like Cervantes does, following Erasmus, that the inner dialogue with God trumps external liturgy? And, besides, he is used to the embellishments that stories suffer when they are told by those who have lived them, my Miguel is used to the twists of memory, the tricks it plays on us. It was a matter, during future visits when she would undoubtedly be accompanied by this invisible and all too-perfect husband Francisco, of digging for details, a bell and call had gone out to visitors to depart, *Closing down, first warning*, he would find a way to tell the tale in such a way, with such fluidity and enchantment that disbelief would be suspended, isn't that what writers do, what Miguel de Cervantes has become adept at?

So he says, "Yes," he says yes to the daughter of Juan Navarra, "yes, you may return here tomorrow, your lady Zahara has sent you to the right person. I will honor your father's memory and write your story."

He does not tell her that he has been warned by his own three men—does it matter if they are the same ones, are not they all identical?—that if he were to engage in this sort of writing, they will come back and interrogate him, they will come back and then they will—who knows what they will do. Who cares what they'll do. To Hell, to Hell with those men and any other men like them, the thought surges in him as if from a blaze, suddenly returned to who he truly is—is it Cristina's fresh presence, is it the fearless last message from Zahara, is it the specter of Juan winking at him?—whatever the reason, this he knows: he is the son of his own works, and he won't let anyone in this world or the next one turn him into a coward.

Cristina cannot read his mind as I can, but she can read the determination in his face, his readiness to do battle for a woman in distress, as I will, as I would if given the chance.

Another call goes out, *Closing down, second warning*, the jail is shutting down, all visitors must leave or remain during the night at their peril or for their pleasure. "Our gratitude, kind sir," she says, as she proffers a small pouch to Cervantes, brimming with coins. "There is enough in this bag—thanks to the sale, bit by bit, of my lady's jewelry—to see you through the next months of your troubles, find the time to . . ." And here she stands and leans over and it is as if Zahara herself were again whispering in his ear: " . . . time to write, write as if you were already dead, because the dead have nothing to fear."

And before Miguel can reject the money, before he can inform her that he does not require this kind of recompense, that she has already given him something far more valuable than all the treasure in the universe, she is gone. The veil comes back down over her face, those cheekbones and lips of Juan's that live on in her, gone, gone, leaving behind the dizzying magical whiff of Zahara's perfumed soap, she is gone and I am afraid that her absence may hurl him back into the dismal abyss in which she found him some hours ago, that is what eats away at me as even her fragrance, the exhalation of Zahara, dissipates, leaving the stale, sour smell of the prison, and instead of her voice the last call, *Closing down, third and final warning.*

It is late in the day and he is hungry. Clutching the bag he did not wish to accept, he is nevertheless thankful for it. He approaches one of the stalls and is rewarded with a steaming bowl of fish broth and hearty bread. A wondrous soup to culminate a wondrous day! Sustained by the food as much as by the encounter, he mounts the steps towards his cell on the second floor, passing by prisoners who remind him that he is expected at the infirmary this evening, that they missed him yesterday and await another reading session with bated breath, step by step, prisoner by prisoner, he goes up to this cell where pen and paper await him.

He knows how to start the story of Ahumada, he wants it to sound different, to catch the attention of the Privy Councilors to whom he will address the long letter, stimulate their interest with a mysterious beginning, the hint of something mythical.

I tremble as he writes: "Somewhere in the mountains of León, there is a town whose name I will not reveal yet, where my eyes first saw light and ... "

And ... and ... and another sort of light is failing in the cell and the day has been exhausting and the memories weigh heavily upon him and he cannot help his eyes closing, I myself cannot keep mine open or find the strength to urge him on ...

"Somewhere in the mountains of León ..."

He tries to fight the drowsiness and cannot, nor can I, we are so close to one another now that I am also falling asleep, and once again we go into a dreamless languor akin to death and once again there is nothing there, not an image to salvage when we are awoken, again by a hand on Miguel's shoulder and again there is no one in the cell but Josep Jordán with his flowing beard, white and grubby, and again he is begging pardon, but he waited yesterday all afternoon and today all through the day for his letters and Cervantes did not come, did not even show up at the reading session last night which everybody had so eagerly been anticipating, and if there were not such urgency he would not have wanted to bother but his case is about to be judged and he has paid Papa Pasamonte already and—Miguel stops him, shaken, alarmed, mystified.

"But," he stammers, "I read them to you, yesterday I—" and his good hand burrows into the crevice where he keeps the correspondence he is working on, and there they are, the two letters for Jordán, and what he instantly feels, as before, is relief that those three men—those nasty men—did not ferret them out, but that relief quickly spins into bewilderment, he looks around to make sure he is not still asleep and dreaming this bizarre, impossible recurrence of events he has already lived, he looks for the paper on which he was writing the story of Francisco and Cristina and it has disappeared, he turns to Jordán and cannot help but asking:

"And the lady? Has she come back, is now downstairs?"

"What lady?"

"The lady, the lady with the veil, the pretty one, the one I spent all day yesterday with the lady who left me some—"

And his eyes descend to where the bag of coins dangled from his waist and the bag is gone, the money is not there, could it have been stolen from him while he was asleep?

"There is no lady," Josep Jordán replies. "There are several prisoners lined up to talk to you, sir, but no women today, I would know for sure if one of them was a woman, you can believe me."

"Not from here, not from jail, the young woman that I was—she has to be down there."

The old *alcahuete* looks at him as if he were crazy. "You had a hard time yesterday, sir, with those visitors, you must mean Constanza Salvadora, who—"

"Not Constanza, nothing like Constanza. The lady who gave me . . . she asked me to . . ."

And he looks around the cell and again down at his empty hands, at the absence of the bag with coins or the paper where he had written those words, *Somewhere in the mountains of León* . . . . And he realizes what has happened, I realize it with him, we both understand that it was an illusion, a vision that has vanished, Cristina does not exist and Zahara has sent no message from her deathbed, and we do not have the funds to subsist in this prison, it was a dream.

Maybe he has dreamt it for me or I have dreamt it for him or we have dreamt it together or we have dreamt it separately and coincidentally and simultaneously, but the result is always the same, waking up to the harsh reality of pimps like Jordán and whores like Constanza and bosses like Pasamonte and this jail from which he will not be soon released because of men like those tormentors.

And yet, that dream of redemption persists inside me and I can tell that also inside him, perhaps with even more strength—because everything we touch will soon turn into a dream anyway, life is a dream from which death awakes us and perhaps not even death, perhaps there is nothing on the other side, and on this side nothing but this dream and the next one, but why should what we have dreamt be any less true, why should Miguel not take courage from those last words of Zahara, why can that message not be the one he needs, why can Cristina not have been the messenger he needs, and the wink, the wink, the absolution from the daughter, why does any of this have to be false? Why cannot characters in a dream—or in a book, in a book—be less real than he who dreams them, he who writes them?

And who is to say that Zahara did not send him this dream last night as she died, who is to say she has not been working for all these years to liberate Cristina and a girl like her will appear someday with her *cautivo* husband to tell Miguel their story, who is to say, who is to say? Once again freeing him, allowing him to survive, ransoming him from apathy, the captivity of despair.

Who is to say he cannot send those men to Hell in this prison as he did in our dream, who is to say that he cannot write as if he were already dead, write as if from the exile of death, write from the silence that men like those interrogators know nothing about, who is to say he is not more cunning than them, that he cannot find a way around their threats and their violence and their ignorance, who is to say he cannot show the courage in his art that he showed at Lepanto and during the years of slavery in Algiers, who is to say he is not freer in jail than all those who think they are free out there in the outside world and yet are consumed with dread.

He takes his pen and feverishly jots down:

Somewhere in the mountains of León, in a town whose name I choose not to reveal for now . . . .

No, something else. Something that already stirred inside you while we talked with Esteban Estudillo, I murmur to him, it was there at that moment, don't you remember, don't you realize how close you were to the truth, you still are.

And he seems to listen, perhaps having shared that dream and all that it entails, perhaps having opened to me yet one more chamber of his heart and one more tunnel of his past and one more absolution from the dead, perhaps that has finally created the bridge that will allow me to cross over to him and merge with his voice, he looks at the piece of paper with those words on them, *Somewhere in the mountains of León, in a town whose name I choose not to reveal for now . . .,* and takes up his pen once more as if it were a lance, ready to continue when ... that is the instant—no, I can't believe this!—that Papa Pasamonte chooses to stride into the cell.

His colossal protector waited for Miguel last night in the infirmary with all the comrades, the thieves and murderers, the *alcahuetes* and sodomites and counterfeiters, and also a few of the falsely accused. Pasamonte patiently explains that he and his friends understood that yesterday's meeting had been stressful and so made no demands, allowed their author to sleep away the night and most of the day, but now, now it is time that he honor his contract, it is time to read to the inmates, each of whom has paid a fee, each of whom would not take it well that Cervantes renege on the agreement they have reached, especially tonight, as the novel he has been reading to them for several months has reached its final chapter and for some of the men it is their last chance to find out how the story ultimately ends.

"But first my two letters," says Josep Jordán. "I need to approve them, get them sent today—then the session."

"Right," agrees Pasamonte. "Your letters first, then our session."

The session, the reading session! I also missed it, had been anticipating the occasion. A major difference of opinion with Miguel. Ever since that first sitting when, for several hours, he has been forced to read out loud to that illiterate audience those books he finds mendacious and superficial, he has not ceased to complain to Padre de León that he is bored by those stories, while I gorge on those flights of fancy, losing myself as the listeners do in the marvel of such adventures. So I always encourage him to look forward to these events: if the literature itself does not amuse you, I have said, at least enjoy the company and the discussions about the characters and the plot. But that's not the message I send him today. Today I yearn for Cervantes to stay here in our cell and keep writing.

I say to him, almost rudely, as loudly as I can: Just ask Pasamonte for a delay, a postponement. Forget the supplemental income, no matter how crucial it may be now that the bag of coins has evaporated along with our savior Cristina. Forget everything but what matters, that blank piece of paper waiting to be filled with the words I have been thirsting for since I made my appearance in Valencia the day you returned to Spain and to this language, words that only now, having fully heard them, can I recognize. Cervantes shakes his head, whether in dismay, or out of weariness, or to rid himself of my pesky voice inside.

He looks longingly at the piece of paper that he will have to abandon, at the pen that is poised to persevere, he sighs and takes the two letters and reads them to Josep Jordán, just as he has done in the dream, engages in the same dialogue regarding how obdurate judges might favor him, except that this time the old pimp does not end the conversation by mentioning that a lady is waiting downstairs, there will be no aroma down in the courtyard, no veiled Cristina, no story of captives making their escape, no deathbed message from Zahara, only Pasamonte who is standing there impassively, arms crossed, unwilling to let Cervantes off the hook.

And thus it is that both Miguel and I walk out of the cell, leave behind us the unfinished phrase that could be the key to our future, and slowly mount the stairs behind Pasamonte up, up to the infirmary.

And only when I see that group of men, only when I see the book awaiting the voice of Cervantes, only when he greets them and starts to read today's selection, only then does the earthquake of a revelation shake me, only then do I understand that this is the best possible thing in the whole world that could have happened to us.

SEVEN

"The truth be told, esteemed friend, that due to its style this is the best book in the world: here knights errant eat and sleep and die in their beds, and make wills before their death, and everything else that in all the other books of this genre are missing."

—*Don Quixote de la Mancha*

FOR A GOOD while today's session is not any different from that occasion, almost four months ago, that first time he had read a book to an assembled company of prospective listeners.

Back then, that night in September of last year, the weather was mild, he and I imagined the breeze outside in the streets of Sevilla that were forbidden to us now that we were imprisoned, as was forbidden to us the sight of the leaves of the trees starting to turn brown, how we would have loved to have felt the coolness blowing from the river. Especially because there was nothing mild or cool about the atmosphere Miguel encountered when he walked into that room for his inaugural experience in reading to the inmates, who were more belligerent than anyone could have foreseen.

Indeed, a red hot battle between two acerbic groups had been in progress, a dispute that had been briefly interrupted to greet the new reader, Miguel de Cervantes Saavedra, to be renewed again instantly with even greater gusto. One group insisted that it was imperative to begin reading the second part of *Don Belianís de Grecia*, which continued the adventures of that invincible knight and introduced his even more valorous son Belflorán, while the opposing group demanded to hear *Las Sergas de Esplandián*, which featured the unequalled male off-spring of the extraordinary Amadís de Gaula.

The quarrel wasn't really about the books—none of these prisoners knew how to read—but rather about which of the two, Don Belianís or Amadís, was the greater hero. A disagreement that extended to their respective ladies, Florisbella and Oriana, adding to the mix, for good measure, the magicians who accompanied the protagonists, one camp extolling the incantatory powers of Urganda la Desconocida, always eager to help Amadís, and the other, the supernatural faculties of Fristón, the sworn enemy of Don Belianís. And the comparisons and disparagements flew this way and that, encompassing the squires who accompanied each knight, and the lands from which the favorites came, and the territories they crossed in search of virgins to rescue and orphans to shelter, *jayanes* to subdue and tourneys to win.

And I had been, back then in September of last year, about to give my own opinion—which they couldn't have heard anyway, though perhaps it would have influenced Cervantes in some indirect way—when Papa Pasamonte, who, we were to discover, always remained neutral in these competitions in order to legitimately intervene if violence, as was often the case, erupted, began to scold the rival gangs for wasting the time of their new guest and the money that they had paid for the privilege of having him read to them, concluding with the dictum that the matter was best resolved with a vote, each listener with one say in the matter, because when God sends dawn he sends it to all.

A goodly solution if the two parties had not divided evenly, twelve and twelve—like the twelve peers of France, said one group, countered by the other that affirmed it was like the twelve knights of the round table, and they would have started yet another quarrel regarding which of these ancient warriors had sallied forth on a more noble quest, if Alonzo Ballesteros—yes, there he was, the first client Cervantes had written letters for—had not belatedly entered the room and cast his vote with the devotees of Don Belianís. Some of the fanatics of Amadís and his son Esplandián grumbled that it wasn't fair for this Ballesteros to decide what they would be listening to, given that he would be strung up and hung three days later and they would be forced to abide by his choice for many months. Pasamonte decreed, however, that this was not an argument worth advancing, seeing that most of them would soon also fade away from the midst of this assembly, either because they had been executed or sent to row in the galleys or even, in a few cases, deemed innocent of the crimes they had been accused of. Whereas he, Papa Pasamonte would remain here permanently, along with the gatekeepers old Ginés and the scruffy, devious Urbaldo Rojas. So, he got to decide and, imposing his iron-fisted rule, decreed that the vote of Ballesteros be tallied and the voice of the majority accorded respect.

And so, the whole company had settled down. Even those uncomfortable with the resolution were anxious to find out if this Cervantes was any good as a reader, gladdened when he had proven himself to be most excellent, more than equal to the epic task.

"Here we commence," Cervantes had stressed each word clearly as he opened the first page of the novel, enjoying at least his own voice, trying not to convey his amusement and perplexity at the literary wrangle he had just witnessed, that those characters seemed to have more weight of reality for these men than their own lives, "composed by Gerónimo Fernández, the New Book of the Valiant Prince Don Belianís of Greece, in which many and diverse adventures are recounted, among which the freeing of the Princesses who were taken from Babylonia."

"Yes, yes," from a chorus of the followers of Don Belianís, "didn't we say it, didn't we say that this would be resolved?"

Before the detractors could respond, Cervantes had rapidly persisted: "The previous part of this *Historie* relates how, in pursuit of the princesses who were forcibly taken from Babylonia, many princes and knights set off, and that the lofty and valiant princes and rivals Don Belianís of Greece and Ariobarcano of Tartaria journeyed together. Well, now you must know that in their hearts friendship had lodged and changed them so that Ariobarcano desired the content of Don Belianís—"

"Don't trust him," shouted Urbaldo Rojas, the unpleasant gatekeeper who was wearing the frayed shirt he had stolen the previous day from Cervantes.

"Rivals can become friends," retorted old Ginés. "Look at us. Look at the women I've procured for you, even if I favor Amadís."

"Gentlemen, please," Cervantes said, and continued: "In spite of all the contrarieties they had been through, they both together sallied forth into the sea with only their squires, without any certainty of the road to be taken, with so much sadness due to the loss of the princesses, that they could not guess where they were heading nor, if they did know, would they have cared at all. Above all, Don Belianís who, remembering to what point his happiness had reached—"

"He shouldn't have waited all those days before marrying Florisbella," a thief interjected. "What do you know about such festivities!" replied Alonzo Ballesteros. "Florisbella, like my wife Amanda, perhaps soon to be a widow, merited every feast and tourney in her honor. She wouldn't have loved Belianís if he had not followed tradition, as we always did in the Army."

"Oriana would have loved Amadís no matter what he did! And Amadís would never have let that flying chariot even near his beloved."

"Amadís would never have been able to rescue someone like Florisbella. He spent half his days crying and whining."

"Crying and whining! That's what you'll be doing once I show you what a true knight is made of."

Lest Alonzo and his rival turn their insults into real knives and steel, Cervantes plodded on, hoping to placate them, as if he were Orpheus, with the music of the next lines: "There was nothing Don Belianís saw that did not doubly increase his distress, though it came to pass that one night when the sea showed itself to be placid, its waves swaying with the temperance of the air, he rose from his bedstead and sensing the serenity of the sea and how scant was the repose that his soul possessed, he cast himself prostrate against the castle of the stern, forgetting all the great deeds he had accomplished with so much honor, in a murmur and low voice so the sailors would not hear him, he began to complain, telling of his many misfortunes, and swearing and promising to kill Perianeo—"

The crowd back then in September had greeted this promise with alacrity. "Kill him," a refrain cried out, "cut that treacherous, felonious knight to pieces" with opinions filtering across the room, with such vehemence that the lights of the candles flickered, "Don't trust that one, oh if I had him here I'd show him a thing or three . . . that Persian bastard, I'd show him how a true knight defends the faith!"

Cervantes smiled at their unanimity, was pleased that at least they were in agreement as to the destiny the villain deserved, and though he knew that the next words would break this truce and spread yet more dissent, he pronounced them anyway: "And also to kill the magician Fristón, who was responsible, according to what Don Belianís understood, for the terrible things that had befallen him."

In effect, a fracas had immediately ensued regarding the abilities of Fristón and whether he would end up, as one group suggested, as the friend of Belianís or whether he was destined to be an enemy forever, a spat which somehow derived into a discussion about the scars suffered by Don Contumeliano of Fenicia, scars so widespread and ferocious that Don Belianís, disguised as a woman in order to escape captivity, would not have recognized him when—

"Enough!" Papa Pasamonte had roared. "We are gathered here at the sacred altar of chivalry, in order to hail the feats of these paragons of our human kind, and not to be bored to death by your inanities. What will our honored Miguel de Cervantes, just arrived in our merry company, think of us and our reading choices?"

What he thought of them and of their infatuation with those books was something that Papa Pasamonte never discovered. I knew, of course, that my author held those novels of chivalry in low esteem, considered them to be false and predictable, vacuous and artificial, lamented the chaotic sprawl of their meandering structure, the trite and repetitious formulas, the misplaced and bombastic vows of the tiresome and indistinguishable protagonists, he detested how evil was emptied of any meaning by making it so easily overcome and chastised, how conquering fame in the eyes of others was more important than the glory of knowing one's own self and the monsters that abide in the heart, disparagements that, as I could have mischievously pointed out, did not stop Miguel from relishing these romances year after year, spending money he did not have in acquiring every one of them available. And he might not admit it, but he delighted in the disruptions and comments of the sessions—because there were many, despite Pasamonte wielding his knife to keep order—indeed, my Miguel had some cloaked fondness for the adventures he fed those listeners night after night, chapter after chapter, week after week, even if he protested the contrary to Padre de León, even if he excoriated those books of chivalry for presenting fraudulent heroes to the public when Spain was so desperate for real ones, even if the only veritable enchantment of existence, he said to Pedro de León, lies in the lives of ordinary men and the prose and verse of extraordinary writers and not in the hands of idiotic wizards and witches and errant and erroneous knights.

That was not the opinion of his listeners. They have maintained from the start a level of enthusiasm only comparable to mine—though hardly any of the original throng still remain. Over the last months, other ruffians of a similar ilk have

replaced the brigands and pilferers, forgers and blasphem-
ers, each arrival quickly recruited to side with one of the two
groups, pro-Amadís or pro-Belianís, but all of them ultimately
cheering on during the session itself the chosen hero and his
mates, sighing at his troubles and acclaiming his many victo-
ries, all of us embarked together in that riveting novel where
justice was done over and over again and the powerful were
chastened by men armed with nothing more than a sword and
a noble ideal.

Like those illiterate men, I was enthralled. Like them, I
have awaited the end of the story of Don Belianís, somehow
vaguely supposing, without quite understanding why, that
it would coincide with my own full birth, my own chance to
shine like the protagonist.

It was a strange notion, almost like a prophecy, that had no
rational basis in reality, and yet I could not shake it from my
mind, the insight that when the adventures of Don Belianís
end, mine can and shall begin.

And now, on this night of January 6th, 1598, we have come
to the last chapter of the book he started shortly after he
arrived in this jail, now, on this day that commemorates the
Magi bestowing gifts on the infant Jesus after a long journey,
my intuition that something momentous is on the verge of
happening settles into the certainty that I am also about to
receive my gift, my recognition, my reward.

I cannot contain my excitement, even when he begins to
read lethargically. I understand that his mind is on the pen and
paper in his cell, inhabited still by those words, *En un lugar de
las montañas de León*, somewhere in the mountains of León,
en un lugar, en un lugar de . . ., but don't worry, that phrase will

be there for you when you return, I say to him, go ahead, let's finish this book of Don Belianís's adventures once and for all, now that we're here, let's go, just trust me, just trust me that something special is about to happen.

I am not sure if it is because he does indeed trust me, but nevertheless he starts to read. Though without great enthusiasm at first, he drones on about the boasts that a multitude of *caballeros* are dispensing to each other as they assemble for a tourney before they set off to another of their interminable wars, this time against the Egyptians and the Ethiopians and the Amazons led by the unconquered Queen Zenobia. The first three knights forbid their companions and rivals from wearing a feather, a gold shield, a golden sword when they compete, but the vows quickly escalate into ever more absurd and extravagant tasks and triumphs, Rindaro promises to give the kingdom of Nisenia to anyone who throws him from his horse, and Salisterno swears that, after knocking down one hundred adversaries, he will force each and every one of them to ask permission from his lady before bowing to the sultan who is hosting them, and Adamantes cannot swear anything because he is captive of his lady Dolisena and asks if someone will defend his good name, and Brandaleón consents and declares he will capture one hundred horses from under the other knights without using his lance or mounting a steed, and Furibundo, that daring pagan, counters that he will win all the prizes in the jousts, until Belflorán, son of Belianís, tops them all by saying he will defeat everyone so thoroughly that each lady will have to give up the most precious ring on her finger and he will cut off the left hand of each knight and furthermore will capture every last banner in the upcoming war. And so it goes, Cervantes tries to inject some verve into the narration and does not quite manage it until he reaches the end of the endless chapter and then, as the knights get ready for the tourney and the subsequent battlefield, his voice becomes slightly more animated as I get more and more stirred up, he is infected by my fervor, the moment is coming, I can feel the shift in my fortunes as the book comes to its conclusion:

What happened in this strange adventure during the astounding wars with the Nubian princes and the freedom gained for the princess Belania, with what transpired to Florimán, the lost son of Belflorán of Greece who was being brought up secretly in Tartaria, and the fate of the hidden princesses Primaflor and Dolainda and how the fortunes of love of Don Doliflor and Polisteo turned out, these and other great feats I would very much desire to recount, because in the aforementioned tourney each and every one of the knights kept their vows without dishonoring their companions and now, now the voice of Cervantes rises with something akin to elation as he reads the final lines of the novel: *but Fristón the magician swore he had lost the manuscript when passing from Greece to Nubia, and returned there to find it. I have waited for him in vain and he does not come, and to deceitfully continue on my own such an esteemed Historie would be dishonorable; and thus, do we leave this story unfinished, giving license to anyone into whose hands such a continuation may fall to add it to the present chronicle, because I crave to know how it ends.*

Cervantes closes the book with a thud.

"And that's all there is, gentlemen. Finis, finished, the end, it's over."

There is a moment of stunned silence.

Then a rumble spreads, not one group or the other but both of them together, unanimous in their dismay, *What? How can it be? Not true, not true! What happens next? Who will find the child Florimán and who will rescue the princess Belania? No, no, no,* they begin to curse this Fristón who has lost the manuscript and cannot find it and does not return with it to the author, depriving the listeners of what befell the flower of fealty and valor.

Not even Pasamonte is able to calm them down. Only Cervantes could do so, only Cervantes can accomplish such a deed, to be memorialized perpetually in the annals of literature. Because now my Miguel, noting the consternation of an audience that he loves intensely, for whose members he has composed letters of farewell and endearment, these men and so many others who have told him their most intimate *deseos y pesares*, now he offers them a solution:

"Gentlemen, peace, gentlemen. I take it upon myself, and swear by my own lady whose name I dare not pronounce, that when I regain my freedom, I will seek out Fristón's manuscript and have it published, and if, as I fear, it cannot be retrieved, then there is still hope, my friends. Because I have heard that a certain morisco historian—" Cervantes pauses and snatches a name out of nowhere—"the venerated, albeit not always reliable, Cide Hamete Benengeli, has written the saga down and it should not be impossible to track down his work in some market or other, nor difficult to have it translated by a man who was captive with me in Algiers and spoke both Arabic and Castilian. It is my hope that you are all well and alive when that book is published and can have someone read it to you and when that happens and you and the world discover how the grandson of Belianís and Florisbella was brought up without knowing his identity, and finally became a more renowned knight than his father Belflorán and even defeated him in combat under a helmet that concealed his features and then slew many dragons and outwitted many a wizard and banished himself, hermit like, to a desolate spot in penitence for his lady's neglect, all of this and so much more will be in the book and when I have completed this task, I ask for no other payment than a prayer from you, wherever you are, I entreat you to ask heaven to look benevolently upon this author who only wishes to please and educate and entertain."

And as he speaks and as the credulous men applaud and celebrate and thank him, he wonders whether what started as a joke could be the harbinger of something else, considers the possibility of completing the last part of this chivalrous cycle on his own, perhaps make some money from this enterprise, though he immediately dismisses the idea, he would not want his name associated with such absurd fantasies. The idea comes back, however, once he has said goodbye to the assembly, embracing with special fervor those sentenced to death or exile, only once he receives his remuneration from Papa Pasamonte does he revisit that bizarre notion, it grows as he leaves the infirmary and walks along the corridor and down the stairs and the coins jangle as if calling greedily to him.

Why not? Why not write one of these books? Divesting it, of course, of all that is excessive and mystifying and impossible, but then what what would be left? If he brought it closer to home, to his own experiences on the dusty roads of Spain, could such an experiment even be deemed a book of chivalry, find a printer? Who would be its protagonist? What crazy name to baptize him with?

And decides, again, that such an initiative is not feasible, how could adventures depicted in a book like Amadís or Don Belianís occur in, say, Andalucía or Asturias or La Mancha for that matter, no, no, no, he is meant for better things, that is not how he will settle his debt with those left behind, make something of the life that was given to him, write as if he were already dead, write as if he had nothing to fear.

But I am waiting for him in his cell, I am waiting for him inside the ink of his pen and the waters of his mind, I am the miracle he is awaiting, I am here and this time he will listen, this time he is ready.

He has been preparing for this moment all his life. For this, he had to spend those years away from home and endure that long captivity where he learned that in order to survive he had to deceive others, never say what he was fully thinking or feeling or meaning, lie to everybody but himself. For this, he had to return to a crumbling country that did not recognize him nor value his service. For this, he had to write plays and poems and a pastoral novel that nobody really cared about. For this, he has been unhappy in love and marriage, unable to stay in one city or town or village for too long. For this, he wandered the byways of Spain, getting to know its people, its taverns, its humor, its wine. For this, he was jailed a first time in Castro del Río and yet again here in Sevilla, so he could listen carefully and write down all the pain and hopes of the persecuted of the world. For this, Papa Pasamonte demanded that he make the universe smile and Pedro de León tried to dissuade him from devoting his energies to picaresque misadventures. For this, he had to journey into the underworld of dreams where the dead and living meet and everything is possible.

Until it all came together, every piece falling into place, over the last two days. Each and every foundational experience decisive, these and who knows what secret other ones that he does not reveal to me, and yet each one insufficient, by itself, to bear fruit.

Not enough, Miguel, to meet a lunatic who went mad reading books about shipwrecks and lost loves and captivity. Not enough to have those men, the representatives of your nation and state, dash forever the illusion of heroism that has sustained you since childhood, mock its possible resurrection. Not enough that you should despair and forswear writing, lapse into hopelessness. Not enough that your courage was reborn in a dream that had more truth in it than the jail you awoke to. Not enough to receive absolution and a wink from Juan Navarra, in his name and in the name of Alicax and in the name of all those whose undelivered letters have been burnt and forgotten. Not enough that you were contacted by the woman who saved your life and now, with her final message, has saved your captive soul.

Everything falling into place, each piece insufficient but necessary. Opening you to the possibility that came upon you just now, as you read the final page of a book of chivalry, that perhaps an adventure of that sort could be written for our times.

Opening you finally to hear my voice and imagine my sad countenance and make me immortal. This time, this time. This time you light that one flickering candle and sit by it and stare at the blank piece of paper, this time I whisper back to you from within its margins, this time you cannot help but listen. Because I know who I am, who I am destined to be. Because you write: *En un lugar de* ... and then nothing else and wait for my words which are your words: *La Mancha*, I say, *Somewhere in La Mancha, in a place* ...

And I watch Miguel de Cervantes write down those words, *Somewhere in La Mancha, in a place whose name I have chosen to forget*—No, he crosses out the last words, writes instead *de cuyo nombre no me quiero acordar, in a place whose name I prefer not to remember,* and continues, *not long ago, there lived an hidalgo by the name of*—And wonders if he should immediately explain that *the accounts and biographers differ as to what the real name of our hero was.* No, that should come later. *There lived an hidalgo by the name of Quijano*—no, *Quijada*.

How long have I waited to hear these words? Not knowing them in advance but knowing that I would recognize them, as he has, when they came. The words, the name, the place I have been waiting for.

His miracle and mine.

Why then this terror, why not joy at the coming of the dawn?

I am about to be born.

I am about to be born and suddenly realize that this voice of mine that has guided him here, towards my conception, this voice—always only on loan—will disappear into his story, transfigured into something or somebody else. What I have been urging him towards since I surfaced that morning he kneeled down on the beach of Valencia, what I have been pushing and preparing him for, oh I am most fortunate, few characters can be as blessed, and yet, and yet, like all new born creatures, like all the dead, I will remember nothing, once I resurrect in his pages I will not remember even these transitory words with which I vanish, these syllables of my becoming will be swallowed and forgotten.

My first quest is over and a new quest, next to my Maker, is about to begin. As Miguel de Cervantes Saavedra writes out the first lines of his new novel, the time has come for me to say goodbye. The time has come for me to seek out my true self.

After darkness, light. I have to believe, if I am really brave, that after darkness, there will be light.

EPILOGUE

"Since human affairs, particularly the lives of men, are not eternal and are always declining from their beginnings until their final end, and since the life of Don Quixote had no privilege from heaven to stop its natural course, it reached its end and conclusion when he least expected it, because whether it was due to the melancholy caused by his defeat or simply the will and orders of heaven, a fever took root in him and left him in bed for six days . . . and then, surrounded by the compassion and tears of those present, he gave up the ghost, I mean to say, he died."

—Don Quixote de la Mancha

AND YET, I am afforded the boon of returning one more time.

I am allowed by the gods to be with him at the end, on that April 23rd of 1616 in Madrid, I am with him as he was for me when I died. And yet aware, both of us, that he has only this one life to live and this one death to die, whereas I will live again each time a reader opens the pages of the book I inhabit, that I will die over and over when that reader reaches the conclusion, sees me awaken from the fever of my glorious insanity, grieves as I fall ill and make my will and say goodbye to those who loved me and especially to my dear Sancho Panza.

And so, my Cervantes lives on in me, his creature, and I die with him, my creator, *cautivos* of each other, Miguel and I, captives of a humanity that mourns his absence and celebrates my enduring name, forever bound to each other in love and fire.

Keeping you company in the gathering dark.

ACKNOWLEDGEMENTS

"Among the greatest sins that men commit, though some say it is pride, I say it is ingratitude."

—*Don Quixote de La Mancha*

WRITING, AS CERVANTES confirms during the course of his imprisonment in *la Cárcel de Sevilla*, is the fruit of solitude, forged in a struggle to make sense of a world full of chaos and clamor. But he also learns—at least as I have conceived him— that his struggle, lonely as it may be, is incessantly nurtured by multiple others, a generous community that accompanies, at times inadvertently, at other times quite consciously, his creativity.

Cervantes himself never wrote an acknowledgment in any of his books, only praise and sonnets for obscure noblemen who are named, not because they had contributed one iota to the literary work in question, but because the author hoped that these grandees would become patrons who might (he was, alas, wrong) alleviate his poverty.

I am fortunate to live in a different age, where I need not fling accolades to those in power (most of whom would probably not approve of my writing, anyway) and can, instead, recognize some of the people without whom *Cautivos* would not have been possible.

I start, as always, with Angélica, wife, companion, partner and endless reader and corrector of my large blunders and small aberrations, both in English and in Spanish. She encouraged me when I was so often lost, unable to find my way out of the dark places where the characters had transported me. There is a reason why this book, like so many others I have penned, is dedicated to her.

I am grateful, as well, to Suzan Senerchia, our friend and my assistant, who was assiduous in her quest for the materials on the life and times of Cervantes that were crucial to the research that grounds this book in history. She was seconded by the librarians at Duke University, always willing to go the extra mile to obtain the extra document.

My agents at the Wylie Agency, Jacqueline Ko, Jennifer Bernstein and, also, Emma Herman, have been fiercely supportive of my work and managed to find the right editor to rescue from oblivion and indifference my take on the travails and glories of Cervantes as he labored to listen to the voice of Don Quixote.

That editor was John Oakes, who made this work so much better by his judicious suggestions and good cheer. Having already collaborated with him on two volumes of nonfiction that OR Books had brought out, *Homeland Security Ate My Speech* and *How to Read Donald Duck*, I was looking forward to encountering his expertise on the quite singular field of fiction. My greatest pleasure was how John *recognized*, deeply understood, what *Cautivos* was trying to accomplish. My appreciation also goes out to OR's managing editor Emma Ingrisani, whose love for literature was amply expressed in the care she took of this book on its way to publication.

Thanks also to our friends, Miriam Cooke and Bruce Lawrence, who provided me with Koranic guidance and wise phrases that still resonate with me today, as I assume they did for Miguel all those centuries ago. And Deena Metzger and

Max Arian, thanks, as always, for reading first drafts of the manuscript and offering clarification and reassurances that I was on the right path.

One of the most heartbreaking experiences while writing this novel was to conjure up Cervantes trying to invent his wondrous Don Quixote without the refuge of a family to sustain him. I was blessed to have those who loved me nearby. Without the near and far presence of Rodrigo, Heather, Joaquín, Cece, Nathalie, Ryan, Isabella, Catalina, Kayleigh, Emmy, Ana María, Pedro, Patricio, Marisa, Sharon and Kirby, this novel would still be buried in some prison of my mind.

Thanks to them and to so many other friends and colleagues for helping me give birth to this tale of how Cervantes dared, in the worst of circumstances, to imagine a contemporaneous Knight who was mad enough to set out in search of justice in a world that, back then as now, was in dire need of redemption.

—Ariel Dorfman
October 2019

ABOUT THE AUTHOR

BORN IN ARGENTINA in 1942, Ariel Dorfman spent ten years as a child in New York, until his family was forced out of the United States by the persecution of McCarthy. The Dorfmans ended up in Chile, where Ariel spent his adolescence and youth, living through the Allende revolution and the subsequent resistance inside Chile, and abroad after the dictatorship that overthrew Allende in 1973. Accompanied by the love of his life, Angélica, to whom he has been married for over fifty years, he wandered the globe as an exile, finally settling down in the United States, where he is now Walter Hines Emeritus Professor of Literature at Duke University.

Dorfman's acclaimed work (which includes the play and film *Death and the Maiden* and the classic text about cultural imperialism, *How to Read Donald Duck*) covers almost every genre available (plays, novels, short stories, fiction, essays, journalism, opinion pieces, memoirs, screenplays). In all them, he has won major awards, leading to accolades from *Time* ("a literary grandmaster"), *Newsweek* ("one of the greatest novelists coming out of Latin America"), *The Washington Post* ("a world novelist of the first order") and *The New York Times* ("he has written movingly and often brilliantly of the cultural dislocations and political fractures of his dual heritage").